I0677563

Riding With Ravan

Second Edition

Ezhuth Aani

Myth Publications
Jamaica,
New York
USA

Dedication

This book is dedicated to the armed forces who have sacrificed their lives to guard the Northern frontier. May their services not be in vain and may they inspire more people to rise to protect the nation from its enemies.

Foreword

Sri Lanka is a beautiful country with a mystic subculture that many don't know of. And it is inseparably joined together with India by the legend of Ramayana and also by the Rama Sethu Bridge. Regardless of the political differences Sri Lanka and India have more in common than most of us realize. If this book generates sufficient interest to promote a tourism trail and helps generate understanding between the peoples of the two countries I would have fulfilled my mission.

An Indian family seeking to have an "off the beaten track" holiday find themselves in the middle of an adventure of a lifetime.

What did they find?

This is a retrograde science fiction, a unique genre.

I wrote this novel while watching River Hatea in Whangarei, New Zealand.

This is an updated edition.

Ezhuth Aani

Anantha Ramanathan MD

New York

April 10th 2022

Cover design: Dr Steven Lev MD

1

I wanna pee! I wanna pee!" Ajay screamed at the top of his voice, jumping up and down. It had been a long day for the thirteen year old. He had not had a chance to relieve himself since 6 o'clock in the morning. It had been seven hours. The children were tired and hungry.

"Can you hold on for a little more beta," said Lakshmy. She wanted to go to the cafeteria, about 20 minutes' walk from there. It had been a hot and humid day. Their ordeal started several hours before. They had started from their hotel at 5.30 am. To get the whole family ready by that time she had to get up at 3.30. First her husband Sunil and herself got ready before waking up the children. It is hard to go anywhere with kids she thought. When we went places before they arrived, it was much more relaxing. Now it was getting to a point where the befores and afters of a trip were so nerve wracking that she did not enjoy the actual trips.

"Ok, son. Let's go on that side of the pond," said Sunil. He also needed to go. It was easy for a man. They could go anywhere. Not so for the women. Lakshmy and daughter Kavitha had to wait. "Why can't you boys wait till we all get to the hotel? So selfish of you to delay us further when we all have to go to the toilet," said Lakshmy. This struggle happens with unerring frequency. Everywhere you go, the women have to queue up while the men can go in an instant. And they never understand our problems, thought Lakshmy.

They had been in similar situations in every trip they undertook as family. Even before the arrival of the children, Sunil and Lakshmy had had perennial arguments about this toilet break issue. Sunil simply put it down to women being the weaker species. Well whenever he said that he had to pay for that later!

"Mom we don't have to wait for them. We can go to the restaurant ourselves. Let them finish and come." Kavitha was much wiser than her twelve years.

"No! How can they let the ladies go alone?" Lakshmy was determined to have her way.

"Mom it is broad daylight. Besides there is a crowd! And we have cell phones. Let's walk ahead." Kavitha was nonchalant.

"Dad I can't wait!" Ajay stomped his feet. He wanted to have his way.

"Ok girls lets meet again in the restaurant." Sunil led his son to an isolated stretch of shrubs beyond the other side of the pond. This used to be the Queens' bath.

It had been a hard day for all of them, especially the children. It was a hard climb, on a hot day. But it was worth it. From top of the rock, they had seen the splendour of the lush Sri Lankan plains all round. Then they saw and marvelled at the fantastic and imaginative engineering and architectural feat called the rock fortress of Sigiriya. Rocky outcrops are awe-inspiring. Ajay had been to Uluru in Australia. The rock there was considered sacred by the Pitjantjatjara people. This rock in Sigiriya was not really venerated by the local people in that sense. But it was certainly an out of the world experience for the family. Everyone raves over the frescoes of the nymphs. For Sunil it was the engineering and architectural achievements, clearly overcoming severe logistical challenges, which were impressive.

The majestic rock fortress, built 1500 years ago, featured a terraced garden adorned with beautiful ponds surrounding a big palace atop a 650 feet high granite rock. That is, the rock itself was the height of a 60-storey building. The palace was built on top of that. Not only that, the rock featured a huge pair of lion paws sculptured on a mid-level plateau before the final ascent to the summit where the wonderful upper palace and garden were located. The stairs were sculptured between the paws.

At the base there were many terraced gardens and waterways, including the queen's bath that they made a beeline to, and ramparts and moat. It must have taken a genius to conceive and design a structure that blended beautifully with nature.

Sunil, a civil engineer himself, marvelled at the ability of the ancients. To put this in perspective, the four faces of US presidents carved on the face of Mount Rushmore were 60 feet tall. It took 400 workers fourteen years to complete this, even when they had modern explosives and drills to blast the rock and remove it.

How did the ancient workers scale this rock and build a palace replete with artificial ponds and waterways at this height? How did they haul the building materials atop this rock? Not only that, how did they take food and water to the workers at the summit?

He had always wondered that there must have been civilisations with greater scientific and technological know-how than the present, in the ancient past. Without the machines of today, how could anyone have built those massive structures, which have withstood the test of time? How could they have overcome the challenges posed by the height of the terrain and the magnitude of the buildings?

The Colosseum was built in nine years. The pyramids were built with geometrical precision. Machu Picchu was said to be built to astronomical alignment. Yet we think that science began after renaissance! Sunil thought that after his retirement he would spend time researching the building techniques of the ancient civilisations.

Presently the father and son turned towards the bush and away from each other, and started answering nature's call.

"Look dad! Something shining and strange!" Ajay screamed.

Sunil was startled by this sudden yell. Startled so much that he nearly wetted his pants losing his aim. He was annoyed that his son disturbed him. There are some things in life that give you immense satisfaction. And able to empty the bladder after being 'pump tight' for hours is one of them. No one likes to be disturbed during this period of enormous relief.

"What beta? Why do you have to always shout?" said Sunil, zipping up.

Then he squinted to look at the object that had drawn Ajay's attention.

It was a metal object. It was shiny and looked resplendent in the sun. It appeared to be flat and long. It was hidden in the bushes with heavy overgrowth of shrub covering it. It must have been there for many years at the least. Why has it surfaced now and why did it attract Ajay's attention? He did not know the answer to that. What he knew was that the object had piqued his curiosity. He had to look at the whole thing. He needed to know what it was. His scientific mind would not rest until he knew what this thing was. The thing that disturbed his micturition; the thing that has now become more important than his hunger; and of course more important than the ire of his waiting wife and daughter.

He looked here and there making sure no one was watching them. Clad in khaki shorts and white tee shirt, he could easily pass for a local worker, except for the camera in his hand. Most of the people around on this day were foreign tourists, from faraway places including Japan and China. Sunil's brown skin and moustache made him look like a Sri Lankan. And he did not have a haughty swagger about him that most tourists had. His training in the air force had ensured that he had a smart but not arrogant demeanour.

After making sure no one was watching them in particular he asked Ajay to follow him. "Dad there may be snakes" warned the son. He had been well taught by the mother. More than the snakes Sunil was worried about land mines. This is a country that had been on the throes of a brutal civil war until recently. Though Sigiriya was outside the main war zone, nowhere in this small island was too far from the war. He instinctively took small strides, one-step at a time, carefully watching the shrub for any signs of a mine or any slithering.

The anti-personnel mines had been particularly devastating. Many people had lost their legs. There was one particularly vicious type called Jonny mine. This went off as the person lifts the heel. As a result, it took off a chunk of the heel which rendered the foot useless – and the poor victim invariably ended up with an amputation. Sunil was well aware of the hazards of stepping out in unknown bushes in Sri Lanka. However, he was a curious cat. No amount of caution was going to stop him from examining his quarry.

Slowly he reached the metal object, or the part that was visible over the leaves. He got hold of it with both hands and tried to move it.

"What are you doing dad?" shouted Ajay. He was sure he would get a scolding from mother for being an accomplice in this unnecessary adventure.

"Shh beta. Don't attract attention!" Sunil knew that even though the civil war was over any suspicious activity might lead to arrest. It would give rise to an international incident. He would have a lot of explaining to do to his Indian Air force superiors.

The thing wouldn't budge. It was caught in a heavy overgrowth of creepers and short trees. Sunil had a Swiss army knife in his pocket. He wanted to cut some of the plants at least so that he could see what it was that had generated interest in him. He went to work quickly. After about 10 minutes, he was able to see that it was a thin long piece of metal, perhaps a part of a wing. It was obvious that some of it was buried under the soil. He could not tell the full extent of the piece. Nor could he surmise its exact shape or dimensions. But he wanted to know.

Just then, the cell phone rang. "We are waiting!" said an annoyed Lakshmy. "We are hungry!"

"Ok, we are coming." Sunil quickly returned to the cafe where the other two were waiting. Ajay was grateful that his mom called. He was waiting to tuck into the Sri Lankan hoppers that he had been promised for lunch. Sunil knew this was a big job. He had to come back with help. He just had to know.

When Lakshmy and the kids wanted to spend the afternoon lazing at the Kandalama hotel, Sunil was happy. There was so much to do at the hotel. The swimming pool and the adjacent lake provided ample shelter from the tropical heat. The hotel was landscaped to merge with wild life and nature seamlessly. When Sunil announced that he was going back to the rock to check out something Lakshmy wasn't too disappointed. After fifteen years of marriage she appreciated some downtime away from her spouse. Otherwise, they would be in each other's hair and the vacation would be spoilt.

Sunil took their tour guide, Mr. Fernando, to a side. He said "Look here Mr. Fernando I need a huge favour from you," he started. True to form, Mr. Fernando agreed before even asking him what it was. Sri Lankans are noted for two things. Firstly, they all have a winning smile. No matter what happens, they smile. Even in the height of the war, no one could wipe the smile away from their faces. Secondly, they are helpful. They say yes to any request and genuinely try to help, as far as practicable.

Sunil said, "I saw this metal object in the shrubs near the queen's bath. I want to go back and extricate this from the soil. I want to know what it is."

"Ok sir. Done." Mr Fernando gave his word. That evening when the tourist activity had diminished a bit, Mr. Fernando arranged two villagers to accompany them to the spot where Sunil had seen his metal object. They were able to cut the bush and excavate the whole item, wash it and take it to his hotel room.

2

That night the family invited Mr Fernando to join them for dinner. Tall and bespectacled, Fernando had been a tour guide for twenty odd years. His salt and pepper hair made him look young enough to be a dynamic companion and experienced enough to know the ins and outs of the tourist places of Sri Lanka. He regaled the children with all kinds of tales, from local mythology to history of the country. After dinner, Sunil packed off the children with Lakshmy. He invited Mr Fernando, his accomplice in the new discovery, for drinks. They gathered the neatly wrapped parcel that was given by the villagers and moved to a corner of the bar. Sunil unwrapped the article. It was wrapped in a jute sack. The villagers had actually washed it.

Lo and behold! He took out a piece of metal, smooth and shiny, which was about 4 feet long and 2 feet wide. It was shaped like a blade of a fan. It was three inches thick. It was probably broken near the shaft where it joined the axle, were it in fact a fan. Surprisingly it was very light for its size. Moreover, it was very strong for its light weight.

"What could it be?" asked Sunil.

"To me it looks like a part of an aircraft. Either it is part of an aeroplane engine or it could be part of a helicopter." Mr Fernando was speculating. For all his worldly knowledge, his comprehension of matters relating to aircraft was poor. Sunil was an air force engineer. He agreed whole-heartedly that this was part of an aircraft.

"Have there been any crashes in the region?" asked Sunil. Surely, Mr Fernando would have known if there had been a major incident.

"Several planes were downed during the civil war. But none in this region as far as I know. I remember an Antonov was shot down near Colombo. Another civilian plane was shot near Vidathaltheevu in Mannar on the North-western side of the country. Then we had a few crashes near Jaffna during the war. Two air bases were attacked and several planes were destroyed while grounded. But they were far away from here. Then there were the tiny planes used by the tigers. They all came down in areas well away from here. Unless there were other crashes in the jungle that we don't know about...

"I am trying to think. There was a major plane crash in the seventies. That was the only major incident before the civil war. I am trying to jog my memory. Let me think. I am sure I will get it..."

Mr Fernando was trying to remember the crash that shook a nation. He was a child at that time. It was a horrendous accident. It had kept the newspapers busy for several weeks.

He paused for a moment. He wrinkled his forehead, indicating he was thinking hard, and looked at Sunil, who was waiting with bated breath.

"Oh it was a DC 8. I remember the details now. They were passengers from Indonesia going on a Haj pilgrimage. Nearly 200 people died in that accident. The plane was lower than where it should have been and slammed against the mountain!"

"Which mountain?" asked Sunil. "Sigiriya is too low to be in the way of an aeroplane, surely."

"No. It was a mountain range called seven virgins. It is more than a hundred miles away. Do you think the wreckage would be scattered this far?"

It was unlikely, Sunil thought. Then what is this piece of metal? Could it be part of agricultural machinery? He had never seen anything like this in the farms that he had visited, given that his father was a farmer. Then the equipment was evolving all the time. It was possible that this piece of material belonged to some mundane earthly machine and not a heavenly highflying contraption. Something about it told him that it was no ordinary piece of junk. It intrigued him.

He decided that he needed to get to the bottom of this. He loved challenges. It gave him a purpose in life other than getting married, raising children, amassing wealth for retirement and then, leaving it all and ending up in an incinerator or under the ground. It fired his imagination. It made life exciting.

He was on a two-month hard-earned vacation. He had been in the Kargil conflict. Being the workaholic that he was, he had chalked up a lot of leave, as he seldom took time off for vacation.

This was the long awaited family trip. It would not have come about, if not for Lakshmy's incessant lectures on the need for quality family time, at least for the sake of the children. The kids were on summer vacation. This was a holiday of a lifetime for them.

Sunil decided to take the article with him back to India. He will ask the experts. He just had to know what it was. With Mr Fernando's help, he repacked the item carefully, and took it back to his room. As he carried it he could not but be amazed, by how light it was, given its size and thickness.

As he creeped under the sheets next to Lakshmy, she sleepily murmured "Oh Sunil! I have been waiting here. As usual you spend time with your friends until I am really sleepy!"

Saying this she turned away from him. Sunil lay awake for a little while, and dozed off. In the night, he woke up with a startle! He had a dream where many demons came to pay obeisance to him. It was a vivid dream. The demons were of different colours, red, green and purple. They had big teeth, blood shot eyes and breathed fire. Many had tails. But they did not seem threatening. Rather they appeared to be friendly. They should normally be scary and ferocious. But Sunil did not feel afraid at all. He was relaxed.

He had woken up when Lakshmy tapped on his shoulders and asked what are you talking? She was worried that he had been blabbering to himself.

Well the dream was indeed more interesting than the reality. He was now back in the world where he had to play husband and father to his family. They did not look ferocious but they did not look as colourful and interesting as his dream beings had been.

They fell asleep again, to be woken up by the spreading sunlight in the room and the chatter of the children, who had woken up before them.

"Mr Fernando will be here at 9 am", said Lakshmy. "We need to get ready." The hard task master that he is, Fernando had allowed them a bit of lie in, after the arduous rock climb the previous day. The destination was close by.

That day's agenda was more relaxed. They were to visit Dambulla cave temples. These are the best preserved of the numerous cave temples found in Sri Lanka. This was a collection of at least 80 caves. The caves had been used for at least 1500 years. Probably a lot longer. Nearby pre historic burial grounds indicated human habitation of the area for nearly 3000 years. Of the numerous caves in the area the best preserved five caves contained statues and artefacts of Buddhism. There were also some artefacts of Hinduism. Lakshmy was impressed by how Hindu gods like Vishnu and Ganesha had been incorporated into the Buddhist worship rituals.

Mr Fernando explained to them that during the Polonnaruwa Period a lot of South Indian influence was prevalent in Sri Lanka. Vishnu was especially popular among the Sri Lankan Buddhists. The worship of Vishnu and Avalokiteswara, the prominent Bodhisattva of Mahayana Buddhism, and a version of Avalokiteswara called Natha Deiyyo were incorporated into the local Buddhist culture. According to Buddhism, there is no God. So how do they reconcile themselves with the worship of Hindu Gods? No problem. In typical Sri Lankan style, they found a solution. These are not Gods but elevated Beings, called Bodhisattvas. They help people who seek their help.

For the purist the worship of Hindu Gods may be anathema. It is similar to the worship of saints in Catholicism, which Christian fundamentalists don't approve of. Mr Fernando, himself a Catholic, explained that whatever the beliefs were, there had been religious tolerance among ordinary people in Sri Lanka until recently, even in the face of the ethno political civil war.

The largest of the caves was more than 20 feet tall, which is the height of a two-storey building. There were hundreds of Buddha statues and murals. Of these, the statue of the reclining Buddha impressed Lakshmy the most. She kept raving about the parallels to the reclining Vishnu statues in Srirangam in Tiruchirappalli and the Padmanabhaswami temple in Trivandrum.

The Dambulla rock was much easier to climb. Unlike Sigiriya the incline was gentle. It was much easier for the children to climb. Sunil reflected on the fact that different cultures treat natural wonders differently. For example, Uluru the sacred mountain is not encouraged to be climbed. Here, the people were allowed to climb the rock but they had built shrines incorporating the natural attributes of the rock. Who is right and who is wrong? After all, that is the reason travel makes people more tolerant of others' beliefs.

Another striking feature in Dambulla is the number of monkeys. "Are they Hanuman's people, dad?" asked Ajay. "Do they worship Hanuman like we do?"

"Not really. Remember Hanuman burnt down Sri Lanka! The vanara armies ransacked the country.

Why would they worship Hanuman or his relatives?" said Sunil, trying to explain the differences in the culture between the two countries.

"Bull shit! You are trying to say Ramayana really happened. Those epics are part of our culture and teach us moral values. But that doesn't mean they actually took place." Lakshmy countered Sunil.

"Do they believe in Rama and Sita in this country?" asked Kavitha.

"Good question. I don't know the answer. There don't seem to be Rama temples here like in North India." Sunil said. He made a mental note to ask this from Mr Fernando.

"Well, Vishnu is big here. But Rama and Krishna are not as popular as in India. We are Ravana's people, you know," joked Fernando.

"Ha ha! As if, Ravana existed. You guys are silly." Lakshmy was not one to believe in myths.

"There are many place names and folklores associated with Ravana and some with Sita. But Rama? Not really. He was the invader who stole our princess!" blinked Fernando. He meant Sita was actually a willing captive who did not want to go back to Rama. "Perhaps she had Stockholm syndrome, after being in Ravana's company all those years."

"See what happened after she returned to Rama. She was made to walk through fire. All men are jealous and suspicious aren't they?" Lakshmy played along, taking a swipe at Sunil. Every married couple know about these two way tensions. Fernando did not want to get caught in the middle. So he did not say anything, but smiled big, as is customary for Sri Lankans.

Sunil said "I don't think Ramayana is total myth. There must have been some truth. Otherwise a whole nation is not going to grow up believing in this for thousands of years."

Mr Fernando was neutral. He was a Roman Catholic. So he certainly did not believe in Ramayana in a religious way. Did it happen historically? He had an open mind. If and when he sees proof he will believe it. The jury is still out as far as he was concerned.

3

When they finished at the caves they went to the bazaars. Dambulla was a bustling town. There were many stalls. These catered to the locals as well as the tourists. The children loved the food. They really liked the food items made of kithul hakkuru (jaggery made of kithul palm) and kithul pani (kithul syrup). These were different in taste to the sweets they had tasted in India, which had predominantly cane sugar, cardamom and ghee.

While they were shopping around something caught Sunil's eye. They were the devil masks. Carved in wood they looked like Kathakali masks he had seen in Kerala. But they were much larger and looked more ferocious. They had big rolling eyes and ferocious teeth. There was a big tongue and over the head, there were multiple cobra heads. And he was struck by something. Yes there was s similarity between the demons he saw in his dream the previous night, and the masks in the shops. He could vouch for the fact that he had never set his eyes upon these images before. Why did they appear in his dream? Could he have foreseen today's events in last night's dream? He was confused. He could not take his eyes off the masks. He bought one, much to the disapproval of Lakshmy.

"You are collecting all junk. You picked up some unknown metal fragment yesterday. Now you have bought this huge mask. How will we take them all back to India? There is no room for my shopping!" she lamented. She had planned to buy a lot of sarees on this trip.

"We can arrange for these things to be shipped," Mr Fernando the practical man he is, had seen this situation many times before.

That night the family had arranged to watch a Thovil ceremony, a devil dance. So they had an early dinner and a short nap before getting ready for the ceremony at midnight.

"You are fortunate that we have a patient today. What you will witness is a devil dance to ward off evil beings that have got hold of the patient. By a mixture of rhythmic drumming, fast dancing and chanting they draw out the evil spirit, or yaksha, from the body of the patient, offer him food and incense, and ask him to leave in the name of Lord Buddha and the king of the demons, Wesamuni." Mr Fernando was preparing the children about what to expect.

"Did you say Yaksha?" asked Lakshmy. In Hindu mythology too the name Yaksha was used to indicate supernatural beings. Asuras and Yakshas were supposed to be evil. Gandharvas and Devas were helpful.

"Yes Yakshas are harmful beings. They are trapped in their hatred and reborn in their form again and again. They are trapped in their vicious karmic cycle. Interestingly Yakshas and Nagas are mentioned as the original inhabitants of the island in the Sinhala chronicle Mahavamsa. The father of the Sinhala race, Vijaya, is supposed to have married Yaksha princess Kuveni when he landed in Sri Lanka."

"Wow! Sounds romantic!" chirped Lakshmy.

"Yeah, it was kind of romantic, like the Pocahontas story. But it had a sad ending, as Vijaya left Kuveni for a Pandyan princess," said the guide.

"In any case I just pointed out that the Yakshas that we encounter in the devil dancing may not be really super natural beings. They may be just a representation, of the original people of the land."

"So you think Ravana was a Yaksha?" asked Sunil. He did not know why he thought of Ravana at this time.

"As I said we are Ravana's people. It is possible that King Ravana was indeed a Yaksha and ruled this land long time ago. Yakshas may be just an ethnicity rather than another variety of species." Mr Fernando was proud of the ancient culture of Lanka.

"At least the Yakshas know how to treat their women," said Lakshmy. She never missed an opportunity to say Rama made his wife walk through fire to prove her chastity. By implication, she was saying her countrymen were suspicious people.

Sunil did not take the bait. So there was harmony.

"Do the Yakshas have names?" Ajay had been silent throughout dinner. Now he joined in.

"Oh yes. Wesamuni is their king. He normally doesn't inflict individuals. There are some Yakshas who are more powerful than the others are. Mahasona, Kalukumaraya, Suniyam Yakshaya and Mahakola Sanniya are a few prominent ones. They have their consorts too." Mr Fernando went to town on the pantheon of the netherworld.

"That sounds interesting. Where does Ravana fit into this scheme of things?" Sunil was fixated on Ravana for some reason.

"Oh Sunil, may be you are inflicted by Ravana Yakshaya. That's why you keep coming back to him." Lakshmy had a worried look.

"I noticed that too. Mr Sunil Mishra seems to be obsessed with Ravana." Mr Fernando supported the lady.

"And Mrs Lakshmy Mishra is obsessed with Sita's Agni Pravesha!" said Sunil. Finally, he was able to give one back.

"I am excited," said Kavitha, as they approached the tent erected for the ceremony.

It was a white tent built with poles on four points. The roof was made up of white cloth. Leaves and flowers were tied to the poles as decorum. Soft sand was spread on the ground to facilitate the dancing. The surrounding area was pitch dark, with the time being close to mid night. Flame torches were attached to the pillars of the tent. Some were planted on the ground. The tent was large enough to hold at least 200 spectators around the main arena of the ceremony. The dancers wore red and white traditional garb. Some were bare chested. All wore some headgear. The main actors wore elaborate masks. Then there were drummers and chanters. The master of ceremony, called Kapurala wore resplendent clothes that distinguished him from the rest of the contingent.

The ceremony was impressive. It was a sight to behold! The tourists were given front row seats. The rhythmic beat of the multitude of drums created an atmosphere of awe. The surrounding darkness and the light emitted by the flames created a magical atmosphere. The dancers started slowly but they increased the tempo when the drums started to beat faster. The dancers wore anklets, which added a metallic clang to the low-pitched sounds of the drums. Then came the incense and the smoke. The more they inhaled the strange smell the more intoxicating the whole scene became. The dancers started juggling the flame torches that some had in their hands. Some were able to juggle four and five flames. Now the chanting began. Sunil did not understand the language, which he presumed, was Sinhala. Some words sounded familiar. As is common to most languages in the sub-continent many words had Sanskrit roots. He was able to make out that they were inviting the demons to come out. It appeared that the MC, Kapurala, was invoking the blessings of Wesamuni and Lord Buddha. Lord Buddha being above all the other beings could command the lesser beings to leave the patient. The Kapurala was dancing fast. Some dressed as demons were dancing with him.

Then it happened. The patient who was placed on a low bench got up and started to dance. The patient was a young woman who had been behaving strangely of late. She had been diagnosed with Schizophrenia by the doctors but the parents did not accept that. They thought she was possessed by a demon. Hence the Thovil ceremony.

Why is the patient coming towards me? Sunil was scared. Not only the patient all of the dancers came and started dancing right next to him. Then the Kapurala greeted him and implored him to join them. Why did they select me, thought Sunil. The dancing was reaching a frenzy. They were dancing around him. It looked like they were paying obeisance to him. Sunil was puzzled.

Lakshmy was watching with amusement the dancing around her husband. She thought they were entertaining the tourists. Surely, they will come for tips after making Sunil the centre of attention. She checked her handbag. There were a few five hundred rupee notes. Ok we can give them some money but we need to go to the bank tomorrow, thought she.

Presently Sunil started dancing. Why is he dancing? Lakshmy was very concerned. And dance he did! The children had never seen their father dance, leave alone dance to this fast beat. When they were newly married, Sunil and Lakshmy used to go for discoes in Bangalore. With the arrival of the kids all that came to an end. Even so, Lakshmy had never seen Sunil dance this fast even when he was fifteen years younger. This was crazy! The beat got faster and faster and Sunil did not miss a beat. The young woman danced with him initially in a reverential way but at some point, the dance had transformed into more erotic gyrations of the entire bodies. They were touching each other. Oh my god! Lakshmy was furious. The children did not see any sexual connotations – they were excited that their dad had turned into such a dynamic artiste. Sunil had always been fit but this was beyond anything that they had seen him do in the past. This was supernatural!

As the dancing continued, Lakshmy was getting more and more agitated. And Mr Fernando was also very concerned. Why did they pick on Sunil? He knew Lakshmy was not going to be a happy camper for the next umpteen number of days. And it was going to fall upon his shoulders to keep the peace within the family. Yes it had happened before. During his long career as tour guide he had seen tourist couples fight and fall apart during their vacation occasionally. Usually it was over sexual inappropriateness of one kind or another.

The dancing reached a crescendo, and then stopped! Everything stopped. The dancers had fallen to the ground, with the girl falling on top of Sunil. The drums had ceased suddenly. And the chanting stopped instantaneously. Most of the flames were extinguished leaving only a couple burning. This added to the eerie feeling. The silence lasted a couple of minutes. Then the girl and Sunil stirred. It was as if they were waking up from deep slumber.

Sunil quickly realised his surroundings, and got up dusting off the sand from his kurta and pyjama. The girl distanced herself from this stranger on whom she had been lying. She was shocked at what she had done.

The Kapurala addressed Sunil with his hands together in worshipful posture. He spoke in Sinhala, which Mr Fernando translated. "I have been doing Thovil ceremonies for several decades. But this is the first time Ravana Rajah has visited us during one. Sir must be a specially chosen one."

"What is he saying?" screamed Lakshmy. "My husband is doing dirty dancing with a woman and the guy is talking as though he had witnessed something extra ordinary! These people have loose morals, and have the gumption to rub it in! I want to go home!"

"Calm down Mrs Mishra" begged Mr Fernando. Your husband was possessed by a spirit of some sort. He did not know what he was doing! Besides, aren't you the one who chided Rama for making Sita walk through fire to prove her chastity? Now you are suspecting your man's fidelity!"

Mr Fernando did manage to cool off things.

It was well past 2 am when they reached their hotel. The next day was a holiday from holiday, they had planned. No activity. Just lying in and lazing around. Sunil fell asleep as soon as he hit the bed. Lakshmy lay awake for a long time trying to recollect how closely her husband had danced with that woman. Coming to think of it the woman was much younger than her, and probably more attractive.

4

He did not get up till nearly noon time the next day. His body was aching everywhere. Especially his back and legs were hurting. He remembered only part of last night. It was as though some power had taken over his body. He felt a compulsion to join the dance. After that he did not remember much until he was talking to the Kapurala at the end of the ceremony. It was the weirdest experience in his life. Little did he realise that this was only the beginning of a new reality. That he had come into contact with another realm. Another reality; a reality that was beyond our human senses.

All night he had had dreams, like the previous night. There were demons and other creatures. However, they were not threatening. In fact, they were trying to tell him something. They took him to a place where there was another piece of metal, of just like the one he found in Sigiriya. They were telling him to excavate this. They wanted the outside world to know about its existence. They told him it was on the Northwestern aspect of the rock.

It was just a dream. But the dream had a profound effect on him. Now he was convinced that someone from afterlife or the netherworld was trying to tell him something. Was he to take it seriously? Or was he to ignore it? If he tried to follow his dreams, he will run into a roadblock by his family. Especially his dear wife Lakshmy. He loved her very much. He understood the sacrifices she made to bring up the children while he was away at work. Especially difficult times for the family were during his deployment at the frontlines in

Kargil. Lakshmy had managed the situation deftly. While hiding her own anxieties she had provided the children a very safe secure and stimulative environment, making sure they had all the opportunities in education sports and arts. Now she expected Sunil to play a bigger role in the children's life. They were approaching adolescence and a father figure was very important for them.

He managed to get a transfer back to Bangalore where Lakshmy's family lived and where they had set up home since his marriage. Lately Lakshmy had become bossy and increasingly possessive. She probably felt she had earned this right by giving up her own career as a teacher. She had taken up a role in a nearby school, which was not commensurate with her qualifications. Nevertheless, she had gladly swapped a highflying career for stability. Now she wanted to reap the rewards. The main prize she was after was monopoly over Sunil's spare time. He had his job commitments. That is fair enough. But when he is on holiday she wanted to call all the shots.

In this situation, how can he wriggle out from the family to pursue the orders of imaginary characters that appear in his dream? As it is, Lakshmy was not happy with his dancing the previous night, which she termed 'dirty dancing.' Now if he wanted to go away in the afternoon it would be a disaster for the rest of the holiday. On the other hand, he was really really curious as to find out if there was any truth whatsoever in what the dream creatures were telling him. It may all be just a figment of imagination that has been inspired by the previous day's find. Or he may have stumbled upon something great. He was like a child in a sweet shop that has seen something it really loved on the top shelf in a far corner. If the mother was beckoning the child to come, as they were late for the train, will the child just go or will it risk the mother's ire by making one final dash to grab the sweet?

Well sometimes in life if something is meant to be, things will happen that will facilitate it. So Sunil was pleasantly surprised when Lakshmy ran into Radhika, a childhood friend from her school days. Radhika Nair was a classmate of Lakshmy in high school. She had been best friend with Lakshmy for many years, until they went their different ways. Radhika, who went on to become a doctor, got married and had two kids. The children were almost the same age as Ajay and Kavitha. Unfortunately, Radhika had divorced her husband about a year ago. She had come on a long awaited holiday, after all the traumatic events of the recent past. It was probably the tourist season or perhaps the availability of a number of package holidays; the Indian middle class families were all making a beeline to Sri Lanka.

Having this Paradise Island right next door, Indians had been unable to avail themselves of the great tourist destination for a long time. Firstly, the sixties and early seventies saw the xenophobic Sri Lankan governments tightly controlling the visitors. The fact that the successive socialist oriented governments in India did not leave the Indians to spare much cash on foreign holidays did not help either. Then came the civil war, which took away the better part of thirty years from the country's history. Now with the civil war being over and the Indian middle class becoming affluent, travel between the two countries was at an all-time high.

Having run into her now single friend, Lakshmy was actually happy when Sunil wanted to go back to Dambulla for a second look. As long as he kept off the 'dirty dancing' partner, she was quite content to be left alone with her girlfriend. The children were meeting after a long time and they were having a lot of fun. Sunil hanging around her and her friend would be a nuisance. It could lead to unnecessary after party incriminations! When Mr Fernando offered to go with Sunil, she was doubly happy. He can keep an eye on my man, she thought.

Sunil was delighted at the news of his freedom for the afternoon. Every married man would have empathized with him. Certainly, Mr Fernando knew exactly how he felt. Therefore, when they drove back to Dambulla he asked jokingly "I think Buddhism is growing on you. Are you going to become a monk?"

"Me a monk?" laughed Sunil. "Far from it! I just need an adventure. This holiday is too boring for an air force man!" He then went on to describe his dreams of the previous two nights.

"Well I have never believed in dreams. But after the Thovil ceremony and the way you danced I won't be surprised if someone from beyond the grave is trying to tell you something." Mr Fernando too seemed to have bought in to the story. At his age, he too needed some excitement to keep going at this job. What is the point in showing different people the same things again and again? At least once in a while there needs to be some excitement; some travel off the beaten track, to beat the boredom. Otherwise, life becomes too dreary.

The creatures had said Northwestern region of the rock. The temple and the main cave were on the southern side. Then there was a tank on the eastern side. The North-west was covered in shrub bush. Not many people went there. But some villagers knew about the existence of some caves there. These caves were much smaller than the main caves. In the late eighties when the government violently put down a leftist uprising, there were rumours of mass graves in the area. Moreover, there was talk about ghosts haunting some of the caves. People avoided that side.

"How do you want to go about this?" asked Fernando. He had some shovels and pickaxes ready in the Pajero that they were using. Where do they start and where do they end. That was the million-dollar question.

"If those creatures are real and they really want us to find what they want us to find," said Sunil, "they'll enable us. If they are really supranormal creatures they should have the power to make it happen."

That sounded logical. If they were being guided, all they needed to do was to follow their hunch and have an open mind. The rest should happen on its own.

Serendib is an ancient name given to Sri Lanka by the Arab and Persian travellers. From this arose the word serendipity. Serendipity means fortunate happenstance. Many of the great inventions are a result of serendipity. For example Newton and the apple; But for serendipity to occur the mind of the observer should be open and receptive. Similarly, if they were open to the clues given by the Universe, they would find what they came to find. Who knows, they may be on the threshold of something great. This was Sunil's logic and it was easy to get Fernando to adopt the same attitude. They were like two teen agers on a treasure hunt.

They parked their vehicle in a clearing and started walking on a narrow footpath. They had to go single file. Suddenly it started raining. Just a moment ago, there had been no clouds whatsoever, and now it was totally dark, except for the streaks of lightning that illuminated the skies momentarily, with increasing frequency. The thunder was getting closer and closer until there was a huge blast and a simultaneous flash of light right next to where they were walking. They were already drenched. So there was no point in running for cover from the rain. They needed to get away from the lightning. They could not stand under the trees. They had just seen a tree go up in flames very near them.

"Shall we run back to the Pajero?" asked Sunil. "I think it will be quicker to run under the rock outcrops. We may even find some small cave." Fernando was logical as usual. They were far away from the vehicle. Tthe lightning was getting increasingly ferocious and scary.

"There!" screamed Sunil. Yes, he had spotted a small cave on the Northern rock face. The cave was small enough to allow them to get in only after bending their heads at the neck, and slightly bending their knees. At least it provided shelter. In the state in which they were in, they would take anything. They were prepared to even crawl, if that was what was going to take them to safety.

They made a dash towards the cave. They made it just in time when another bolt of lightning went off just outside the entrance to the cave.

"I should have been a good family man and stayed behind," rued Sunil. "Look what a mess we are in."

"Well there is no point in thinking about what could have been. Now we need to figure out what to do if the rain doesn't stop," said Fernando. He was worried about the rising water level at the floor of the cave. Yes, the cave was in a low-lying area and they had to get to high ground somehow. Going out would be hazardous due to the lightning. Therefore, they had to go in further into the interior. It was dark and scary. Sunil was not afraid for his life. After all, he had been in Kargil. However, he was afraid of the unknown. He was not sure what awaited them inside the cave. This area was full of snakes. He had had two nights of dreams full of demons. The cave was dark. Even the light provided intermittently by the lightning was getting less as they ventured into the cave. He was more shaken than afraid.

Sunil regretted leaving behind his torch. He always carried it but in today's excitement, he had forgotten it. Just then, he saw a small light, coming from where Fernando was. Yes he had brought his torch with him. Sunil was relieved. At least something was working in their favour.

The rain was continuing. Now they could surmise the amount of rain only by the level of the rising water. The water that was at ankle level had quickly risen and they were now standing in knee-deep water. "This is a flash flood," said Fernando. "Unless we reach high ground soon we will be marooned in here." Sunil had had military training. But he was not attired for this flood. Clothed in a pair of casual Denim shorts and a Polo tee shirt, he was wearing a normal pair of shoes. Mr Fernando was in a pair of slacks and a short-sleeved shirt with normal shoes. They were soaked and cold. They had to find a solution quickly in this darkness.

"Look here" said Fernando excitedly. He was pointing to a ledge on the inside of the cave. This ledge was wide enough to accommodate both of them. They knew that if they stayed put they might be at risk of drowning if the rains continued. The rising water forced them to move further in. They realised that the more they went in the more astonishing their findings were. It was in fact a system of caves and caverns joined by narrow tunnels and slits. Some had water. It was hard to judge the depth of water and they had to keep close to the walls.

After what seemed like an eternity, they came to a cave that was dry. This was probably on an elevation. It was actually bone dry.

"Watch there is a snake!" shouted Sunil. Slithering just a few feet away from them was a large Cobra.

"We call it Naya" said Fernando. "We believe that they won't trouble you unless you trouble them."

Well this one must have heard him. It stopped in its tracks and did an about turn, and started coming towards them. "Oh my god it is coming towards us! We don't even have a stick!" Sunil was regretting why they walked into this this trap without any tools to assist them.

The Cobra started hissing and flaring its hood. Somehow, Sunil did not feel threatened by it. Rather he got the feeling that it was directing them to go in a particular direction, into another cave.

Wow! This cave was well lit. There was certainly no gap or fenestration. Where was the light coming from? It was as though the area had been illuminated by a thousand tube lights. The light had a bluish hue to it. It was definitely different to the natural sunlight.

"This must be some magic!" said Fernando. The Cobra had somehow directed them to come here. Why?

"Look there!" Sunil screamed. There on an elevated rock platform within the cave was a metal item, exactly same as the one found two days ago, only this one was complete and polished. Now it was clear that it belonged to a wing or rotor of a flying machine. The piece was able to be lifted and carried easily by Sunil.

Now they realised that the snake had in fact directed them towards this piece of metal. And will the snake lead them out too? Sure enough! It came hissing and did its usual hood spread, making them exit in one direction. Before long, they saw day light through a slit. They realised that they were close to the exit. The way out had been shorter and quicker than the way in.

Once they were outside, the snake was gone without a trace.

Surprisingly it had stopped raining. There was no evidence of flash floods. They had in fact come out on the Northeastern side of the rock. They had to ask directions and had to have a long trek back to their vehicle. Sunil carried his find. It was very light.

When they arrived back at the hotel, it was past 6pm. The sun was setting. Lake Kandalama was beautiful, its waters reflecting the red sun.

Lakshmy and Radhika were seated by the pool while the children were frolicking in the water. They decided to leave their second find in the Pajero. It would not have been politically correct to irritate Lakshmy at that time. Sunil had to break the news about the second load of junk that they had to carry back home. She would surely object to this. But Sunil could minimise the damage by telling her about it later, when she were in a good mood, and they were alone. If she were to chastise him about this, he did not want that to happen in front of Radhika. She was one of her friends that he was quite fond of, and he did not want to be put down in front of her.

"My, my! What have you been up to? You've got mud all over your shoes, legs and clothes!" exclaimed Lakshmy. The boys were always messy. And they don't even know when they were dirty. She knew only too well how untidy Sunil's apartment was, during the times he lived alone. "Go straight to the room. Remember to take the shoes and socks off before you step into the room. Have a shower first. Make sure you don't leave the room in a mess. Put all the clothes in a corner of the bath room." Instructions were flying. Radhika looked at Sunil with a sympathetic smile. He looked at her sheepishly as he went up the stairs.

It was half an hour before Sunil came down to join them, looking fresh and clean, in new clothes. They all had dinner together. Sunil and Fernando recounted their experience at the cave, carefully concealing the fact that they brought back another metal junk.

"Wow! That sounds like a paranormal experience. Are you sure, you are not making this up? We didn't have lightning here!" Radhika cast doubts on the authenticity of the story. Boys always tell exaggerated tales to hide their foolishness. They had got into some muddy mess and now they are trying to impress us, she thought.

5

I am walking out on you if you bring any more of that junk metal!" Lakshmy was furious when Sunil told her. "We come on a family holiday and you spoil it by indulging your own fantasies! When is the last time you have dedicated yourself to keeping the family happy?" Lakshmy was sobbing. All the small things that had been building up over the past few days suddenly came to the fore. The floodgates were open. She said "Oh my god! Why did I marry this man?" Any attempt to pacify her only made her cry more.

"I want you to throw out all that junk you have collected. That includes the mask too. If you don't do that, I am taking the children and going back to India tomorrow."

Sunil had hoped for some intimacy that night. With children around the house, the opportunities for such were becoming less and less frequent. He thought with the children being in the other room, holidays like this offered the best chances. That went out the door with the sobbing bout. Whatever power that was directing his actions did not really care about his sex life, he thought. Must be a frustrated soul from hell. Why am I having to undergo this during what is supposed to be the holiday of a lifetime, he thought. At least that is what he was told by the travel agent. If it was indeed Ravana who was calling the shots then he must be taking out his anger on Sunil, for all the years that Sita rejected his advances.

The next morning he told Mr Fernando about his problems. Before he even broached the subject, Mr

Fernando had thought about it. He had sounded Radhika about the possibility of shipping the stuff through her luggage, as she was returning in a few days and did not have much to carry. She was not into shopping. After the Mishras left, Fernando and Radhika had chatted about various things for more than an hour the previous night. The now single Radhika was only too happy to have some male company. During their conversations, he had mentioned these strange metal objects that seem to be turning up where ever Sunil went. He had asked her if there was a problem with carrying them back to India, could she help. She had readily agreed. She wanted something to beat her boredom. If this is the start of a new adventure, so be it. Even otherwise, it won't hurt to help out a friend in need.

Rather than telling Lakshmy that Radhika was taking them, he just offered to have those items shipped to Sunil. Lakshmy was very happy to get rid of those bulky items so that there would be room for her shopping. The problem solver that he was, Fernando had saved the day one more time.

That day was a busy day. They drove a couple of hours eastwards to Trincomalee. There they first went to Swami Rock, another Sri Lankan rock that rocks. One of the best natural harbours in the world, Trincomalee was coveted by many super powers, including, reportedly, Napoleonic French. It rose steeply from the deep sea. There was one place called Lovers Leap in English and Ravanan Vettu in Tamil. This was a narrow deep-sea inlet where there was very deep sea between two adjacent high cliffs. Legend has it that Ravana's sword fell on this spot causing a deep fissure in the land. Mr Fernando explained that the Trincomalee Bay is geologically a canyon.

"Dad what is the difference between a canyon and a fjord?" asked Kavitha. Sunil answered as best as he could. "Beti I am not a geologist. I know that canyons are formed by erosion over millions of years. It is usually in limestone rock. The best example is the Grand Canyon in Arizona, formed by the Colorado and Snake rivers."

"What about a gorge then?" asked Ajay. "A gorge is a British term. Canyon derives from Spanish and is more commonly used in America. As far as I know they are the same," said Sunil.

"To answer Kavitha's question canyons are found inland. Fjords are formed when glacial rivers cut the rock deeply by their sheer weight and these are found as sea inlets. The sea in between is so deep that large ships can navigate in them. We have seen Milford Sounds in the South Island of New Zealand haven't we?" The teacher in Lakshmy always gives a complete answer.

"Fjord is a Scandinavian term. There are some areas in the world that are famous for fjords. The entire coast of Norway, the Western shore of the lower South Island of New Zealand and the coast of Washington State of USA contain numerous fjords."

Sunil took over. "The sea in fjords is usually called sound. But again the words sound and bay are used loosely."

"Wow! I am supposed to be your guide but you guys have taught me today." Mr Fernando looked impressed.

"That's your reward for offloading that junk from me." Lakshmy was not going to forget about that. She continued, "The beauty of the English language is that it borrows freely form other languages. The words canyon and fjord came from other languages. That's why there is a word to describe almost everything in English. English has more than a million words whereas French has only 100000 words."

"Are you a teacher by the way?" winked Sunil. He was proud of his wife. It showed in his tone. It was obvious from her facial expression that she was pleased with his appreciation. Tonight's going to be good thought Sunil.

Swami Rock housed a very famous and ancient Shiva temple. The great association between Ravana and Shiva worship is well known to all Ramayana scholars.

Close to Trincomalee are the Kinniya hot springs which again is a geological phenomenon but is associated with legends. Having a warm bath in these waters was soothing.

"Ravana is said to have done his mother's last rites here," said Mr Fernando.

"If you mention Ravana again I will have a fit," said Lakshmy, remembering the devil dance and the metal junk the following day. She somehow associated Ravana with Sunil's strange behaviour. Sunil had been normal lately. She did not want him to go off on a tangent again, and spoil their holiday.

"I see your trepidation," said Fernando, with a smile. "You can't come to Lanka and escape the spirit of Ravana."

Sunil wondered whether he meant it literally, remembering his dream creatures.

They managed to reach the ancient capital city of Polonnoruwa late night. The next couple of days were spent in wondrous awe at the ruins of marvellous structures, which have been preserved fairly well over time. If Roman Forum inspired amazement, these ruins should be held in equal admiration.

Mr Fernando explained that the ancient Sinhala lives revolved around the Stupa and the agrarian fields. They built many monuments and religious structures mostly to venerate Lord Buddha. They also built large reservoirs that served irrigation purposes. One of the best-known ancient tanks was the huge Parakrama Samudra, which is in fact three tanks connected by canals. The irrigation system would rival any in the world, for the corresponding period.

"You say climate change is a recent phenomenon. The Middle Ages saw Europe go through a period called Little Ice Age, which was perhaps why the Europeans set out to discover warmer climes. The corresponding period in Asia saw prolonged droughts and monsoon failures. Now don't say I am a climate change denier!" winked Fernando. "It was important to use rain water wisely. These reservoirs were particularly important in sustaining the population."

Climate change had been one of the topics where Lakshmy had been an ardent advocate and Sunil a sceptic. They had had endless arguments over this. Prachuri, an Indian, had headed the organisation that received the Nobel Prize for 2007. This was a matter of pride for Lakshmy. Sunil who had always been sceptical found his voice after Prachuri ran into trouble. Lakshmy, once she made up her mind, doesn't shift her loyalties easily. This statement by Fernando did not endear him to her. But he had helped to get rid of the metal contraption that Sunil was tugging along. She let this one pass.

One of the strange facts about Polonnoruwa was the presence of a couple of Shiva temples in the midst of an overwhelming presence of Buddhist shrines. The contrast in architecture was stark. The square and angled buildings of the Hindu architecture were different to the domed and pyramidal structures of the Buddhist constructions. It was the Chola occupiers who shifted the capital from Anuradhapura to Polonnoruwa, naming it Jananathamangalam. Perhaps the shift after a millennium in Anuradhapura was inauspicious. Though the Sinhala Kingdom reached its zenith under Parakramabahu the Great in Polonnoruwa, it gradually shifted South- westwards in stages until it ended up in Colombo under the Europeans!

Mr Fernando, whose surname itself was a product of the continuous 400-year European occupation of the land, said, "At peoples' levels we don't bother much about who belongs to what religion. We just get along. Can't you see the existence of Hindu temples amidst Buddhist stupas? Peaceful coexistence was what our people were used to until the politicians started to use language and religious bigotry to further their power."

How true, thought Lakshmy. This resonated well with her. Peace at the level of ordinary citizens was important for any society to thrive. She always felt that peace should be a bottom up and not a top down process.

"I want to show you a special shrine," said Mr Fernando." Somawathiya Chaithiya was an ancient shrine built by the father of the godfather of Sinhala nationalism, Dutta Gemunu. Gemunu's father built this more than 2000 years ago. His son Dutta Gemunu was the Sinhala Hero who killed the Tamil king Ellalan, in a one to one duel. This victory was glorified in the Sinhala chronicle, Mahavamsa. Of late, in the last century or so, Gemunu has come to symbolise the ultimate Sinhala hero. Well if you are a Tamil, you may not think so."

Sunil smiled. He knew that Tamils identified more with India, and their heroes were the powerful kings of the Chola dynasty across the straits. What is the point in living in the past, messing up the present, and losing the future?

Somawathiya is built on the banks of the river Mahaveli, the longest river in the island. It is near the area where another large tributary, the Verugal Aru joins it. The area is flood prone and is also a sanctuary for elephants. It is also an area susceptible to malaria. Though Sri Lanka was on the verge of eradicating malaria, Mr. Fernando had advised them to take malarial prophylaxis.

The Stupa was resplendent in white and was awe-inspiring. Mr Fernando explained that Stupa architecture was based on the shape of elevated burial mounds. Most in Sri Lanka were variations hemispherical dome with a conical spire or pinnacle at the top, usually with a square chamber connecting the two. The dome varied in shape with some being bell shaped and others shaped like a grainheap or bubble. The Mishras had never been to a Buddhist shrine before. Sunil wondered why the Buddhists and Muslims built a lot of dome shaped religious buildings. Did this shape have a special power? He had heard that the pyramidal shape confers health benefits to those living under it. Perhaps there are a lot of things that we don't know about, that the present civilization has not discovered yet. May be the ancients were privy to special knowledge.

"Are you wondering about the shape?" An elderly monk approached them. He was smiling with kind eyes. He was looking at Sunil.

"How did you read my thoughts?" Sunil was startled.

"I can read your mind. In fact I can see you are a friend of Ravana Rajah!" The monk looked at him mysteriously. He was tall and well built. He was clean-shaven and his brown face did not show his age. There were some greying hair showing on his shoulders, where his safron robes had not covered him. Sunil thought he must be in his sixties though there were no wrinkles on his forehead.

Lakshmy was astonished and shaken at the same time. Why is Ravana following them? The demon king was supposed to be a myth. Even if he were a historical figure, he should have been long gone. Ramayana, if it really had happened, would have taken place thousands of years ago. These strange things happening to Sunil were spoiling their vacation. Just when she thought it was over, this monk was bringing that up again!

Is it possible that spirits exist? Is it possible that our thought waves can exist in ether forever? After all, they are supposed to be electromagnetic waves. If a recorded speech of Harry S Truman can be played nearly fifty years after he is dead, if Mahatma Gandhi's pictures can be displayed 60 years after he is martyred, if people can continue to live electronically in Face book even after they are well and truly gone, why can't people continue to live as spirits?

The tour was organised by a company called Intrepid Lanka Tours. It was supposed to be an off the beaten track trek. They did not spend a single day in the main cities of Colombo, Kandy, Jaffna or Galle. They were aware of the fact that it was impossible to see all of Sri Lanka in one trip. So they were going on a trail that would take them to some of the mystical under culture. Therefore, instead of going to the main centres they would take a route crisscrossing the land in pursuit of things that a regular foreign tourist doesn't see. Of course, Sigiriya and Trincomalee were the first two stops but now they were going into the deep belly of Lanka to see what the locals see and experience in their daily lives, and some of the things that even regular Sri Lankans don't encounter. But this Mr. Ravana is following them like a third wheel or rather making her feel like the third wheel by hogging the attention of Sunil. She was not happy. At the same time, she was also intrigued about this demon king. One side of her wanted to run away from it all while the other side wanted to see how it all played out.

The Buddhist monk smiled at her. He said, "Ravana Raja is very kind and helpful. He wants to help Sita's descendants. It is very rare that he appears in this world. But your husband seems to be the anointed one!"

Lakshmy was stunned. This elder is reading her mind real time. She can't hide her thought! If only our thoughts can be known by other people just like our words, we will all be in trouble won't we. Unable to hide anything from him and afraid to antagonise him she just stood stupefied.

Sunil asked "Venerable sir can you explain what is happening?"

"I am not privy to the future. But I can sense the presence of our great ancestor, Ravana. It is a once in a lifetime experience for those who are not initiated into these things. All I can say is that you are lucky. You will be protected, and no harm will befall you. Just let things happen and you will be fine."

He then went on to explain about Buddhist Stupas and Buddhist philosophy. It was new to the family, especially children. It was fascinating to know that most of India was Buddhist for many centuries. Now there are very few Buddhists in the birthplace of that religion.

The monk asked with a smile "Are you planning to go to Mahiyangana?" How did he know about their itinerary? Is he getting information from Fernando? Sunil had heard about how some so called 'clairvoyants' were really people who had been able to glean information about their 'customers' from their associates. Fernando did not show any signs of knowing this monk.

"I know what you are thinking. No! I have no vested interests in who you meet or what you do. If you go to Mahiyangana, go and see Hasalaka river. Also make sure you go to Kataragama and look for an Anjanam reader called Sumanatissa. Tell him that Rathina Thero sent you."

Saying this, the monk went away. He did not expect anything from the Mishras. Lakshmy looked at her husband bewildered. Some supernatural power seems to have taken over their vacation. She was one who always wanted to be in control. She hated when she was not in control. She especially hated when Sunil was not under her control. However, here others seemed to know where they would go and who they would meet. She was livid. At the same time, she was curious to see where this Ravana would lead them. May be he was trying to show them his treasure. If there was indeed a treasure trove would they be able to access it? The Sri Lankan government will lay its claim to any treasure found on Sri Lankan soil. So is this all going to lead to nothing? If Ravana is trying to help Sri Lankan government, why has he chosen an innocent Indian family for his games?

The next stop was Mahiyangana. It was an arduous journey through jungle path. Mr Fernando was quite adept at Sri Lankan routes and knew all the stop overs that would make it easy for the whole family. If Ravana was following them, there was no overt indication of this. They had a sense of foreboding. The die has been cast. It was a question of when, not if, the next episode would take place. When fate takes over your life, can you resist? When you give in to the power that is controlling your life a sense of relaxation comes over you. They should just go with the flow and see what happened. Loss of control can be an empowering experience provided you are in the correct mindset.

6

Mr Fernando had chosen Mahiyangana because that would serve as the launch pad in their foray into the jungles of Dambana, where they could meet the original natives of Lanka, the Veddhas. Mahiyangana, on the banks of Mahaweli Ganga, was the site of a famous Buddhist temple, the Mahiyanganaya Raja Maha Vihara. The temple is famous for having had a visit by Lord Buddha. Legend has it that the Buddha flew in to this place to mediate in a dispute between two Naga chiefs. It must have been an air portal of some sort. It is also believed that when Ravana abducted Sita, he first landed his aircraft, Pushpaka Vimana, in a place called Weragantota, not very far from Mahiyangana. When Mr Fernando mentioned that Ravana's aircraft maintenance facility was close by, a shiver went through Sunil's spine. He was sure more surprises awaited him. The demons had stopped appearing in his dreams and he was not sure, when his next encounter with fate would be.

The day passed with no unusual happenings. The children loved the area. It was relaxing and picturesque. This holiday was different. They were actually enjoying the present, rather than tick the boxes and take photographs to post on Facebook, to show friends. The mist covered mountains in the background and the beautiful green planes in the foreground punctuated by lakes and rivers were out of this world. There were many cascades and waterfalls. If Sita was in fact imprisoned in this area, she was one lucky lass. To imbibe in this bounty of nature every day of the year for many years – Lakshmy thought she would have left Rama and stayed here, if she were Sita.

The next day they were to enjoy the nearby Hasalaka Lake and the river. The ecosystem was unique and the bird life was fantastic. The family went boating in the lake. It was a relaxing day. The following day they were to go to Rathna Ella falls. If the children were not there, they could have walked the whole day. With the kids, they decided to go by the vehicle to nearby place and then take the trek of about 3 km by foot.

They set out early in the morning. The early start meant they could catch a glimpse of the resplendent sunrise. They wanted to reach the falls before midday. The roads were slippery from recent rains. The rocky terrain was treacherous and was covered in parts by moss and mud. The trail hugged Hasalaka River.

They wanted to spend a few hours at the falls and return to base early. Planned for the next day was a trip to Dambana where they would meet the indigenous locals. Mr Fernando was particularly strict on time keeping. The weather was good and they should enjoy the trip while the weather lasted. It could change suddenly. Therefore, he wanted to set a brisk pace, get to the area first, and then relax. They carried food and water as well as change of clothes and towels. They also had raincoats in case they were caught out in rain.

The trek was very pretty. Mist covered mountains and the sounds of nature provided an idyllic backdrop. The river was wide in some places and narrow in

others. In some places there was dense overgrowth of
creepers and they had to deviate a bit. On the way
there was a suspension bridge made of rope
connecting two mountain cliffs. The children were
scared but Mr Fernando reassured them the bridge
was safe and securely anchored at both points. It was
still a hair-raising experience, as the planks tended to
move when people walked on them. Mr Fernando
warned them not to look down but Lakshmy couldn't
help herself from doing exactly that. She felt dizzy and
her feet became wobbly. What an experience! It was a
perfect set up for thrill seekers but she was not in an
adventurous mood. After crossing the bridge, she felt
edgy for the rest of the walk. The water was
alternatively muddy brown and green, as the river
made its way through the vegetation under the canopy
of a lush rainforest. There were cascades in many
places but the Real McCoy was elusive. When they
eventually got there, it was well worth it. The gushing
sounds of falling water greeted them on approach.
Here the sound had beaten the visuals unlike in
lightning and thunder. But the effect was equally
stunning nevertheless.

They reached the upper rock pool. The main falls was
just after this. Then there was a pool and a gentler
cascade below. The falls was about 100 meters high,
making it one of the highest in Sri Lanka. Mr
Fernando warned them to be careful. People have
been known to have died in these falls. Unlike the falls
in the Western countries where viewing platforms,
handrails and non-slip wire mesh flooring are erected
to enhance safety of tourists, the falls in Sri Lanka are
generally left as they are. This helps people to enjoy

pristine nature in its wilderness without man made eyesores spoiling the experience. At the same time they can be dangerous too.

"If you want to get into water you have to go down to the pool at the base, as it is not safe here at the upper level," said Mr Fernando. They were just standing by the water at the upper rocks. They had changed into shorts and tee shirts. They were bare footed. They couldn't step in with foot wear. That would make the already slippery surface even trickier.

The water before and after a falls is usually quiet. It is hard to believe that this slow flowing stream would give rise to the falls, which gush down with so much force. How can nature store so much energy in these seemingly still waters, thought Lakshmy. Perhaps if Isaac Newton hadn't wonder about the apple we would still be clueless thought she.

Just then, there was a sudden surge in the water. Perhaps there was rain upstream from the river. Kavitha was standing at the edge of the water. Lakshmy panicked. Oh my god. She was too scared to shout at Kavitha fearing that if she startled her, she may move forward towards the water and be swept away. Silently making a vow to Goddess Chamundi back in Mysore, she moved forward. Goddess Chamundi, if you save my daughter I will climb the hill of 1000 plus steps three times on bare foot, she thought.

Moving forward she was able to get hold of Kavitha and pull her back to safety. But in the process the centre of gravity shifted and Lakshmy lost her footing.

The rocks were very slippery and she rapidly fell into the water. With the momentum of the fall and the force of the sudden gush of water, she found herself moving fast towards the edge of the precipice. She desperately reached out for a nearby shrub but that got uprooted by the force and came in her hand. There was nothing else she could hold onto. She was terrified. The fall would be at least 100 meters onto hard rock. She was sure she was going to die. At least she had saved Kavitha. Even in that panic a serene calm came over her. She had done her duty by her daughter even in her last moment. Her last act was to winch away her daughter to safety.

"Save me some one! Help me!" The whole region reverberated with Lakshmy's screams. Sunil was shocked. He was unable to do anything. It all happened too quickly and before he realised what was happening, Lakshmy was gone.

"Mama! Mama!" cried the children. Everybody was shocked and bewildered. Mr Fernando thought he was responsible for Lakshmy's death. That's it! He was going to stop his job and retire. He had been thinking of retiring for some time now. He had never had a death in his entire career. This was the first time. Let this also be the last time. Why did I bring them here he thought. How am I going to face the family?

The suddenness of the events left everyone paralysed and numb. It was a few seconds before Fernando made the first move. "You take the children to safety. I will walk down the rocks to see if she is there."

Even as he said it, Fernando knew he was actually looking for Lakshmy's dead body. Who could survive this fall? If she did not have a heart attack on impact she would have broken bones, head injury, bleeding wounds...and surely, she would have drowned. There was no more Lakshmy's wailing. There was an eerie silence except for the babbling noise of the flowing water.

If she was injured and still alive she would have been moaning in pain. If she was unconscious she would have drowned. Fernando had a foreboding that he would find her dead body soon. The pool at the lower reaches of the fall was not large and deep like the one at the top. The body should surface soon.

There were a few other people there. They all rushed to help. What can they do? Many reached out for their cell phones but it turned out to be a black spot for all the telephone providers. A couple of youngsters ran to the nearest village to raise alarm. They called for ambulance and medical help. They also told the police. Even for the ambulance, it was unreachable. The last stretches of the road was not motorable. However, whatever help that was practicable was mobilised as fast as was feasible.

A couple of young men got into the water at the lower pool. But there was no trace of Lakshmy to be seen anywhere. Soon a small crowd gathered. Some were pacifying the children while few others were trying to placate Sunil and Fernando. This was an unthinkable tragedy to befall this poor tourist family.
Unfortunately this had happened before. Some of the older villagers said there were treasures hidden under

the water and there were serpents and dragons guarding them. Every now and then, they would exact a sacrifice. Young women were most at risk. So they said.

Sunil's situation was the worst of all. On the one hand, he was blaming himself for not saving Lakshmy. He was angry and frustrated with himself about his helplessness, his hopelessness, and his powerlessness against nature. On the other hand, he thought about the children. How will they take it? How would he raise the children without their mother? How will he himself cope without his dear wife? It was not like he had not seen conflict before. He had been in Kargil. He had seen death and injury at close quarters. It is different when it happens to you or yours. The emotional burden tends to overwhelm you and obscure clear logical thinking.

The children were inconsolable. A few women from the village were trying to communicate with them, and provide some solace even through the language barrier. What can they do? Can they bring their mother back?

Fernando and a few villagers organised a search party. They arranged for people to trek the river downstream to look for any signs of the body or any clothing. The police arranged for a couple of divers to be flown in from a navy camp in Colombo. That would take several hours. By the time they arrived it would be nightfall. For all practical purposes, the body would be found the next day at the earliest. That meant they had to set up camp overnight. The police worked furiously on the logistics. With their satellite phones, they were able to overcome the black holes in the cellular network.

What was supposed to be a nice day's outing for the family had been turned on its head in one fateful moment into a nightmarish tragedy of gigantic proportions. The sun had been a silent witness all along and was now finishing his journey for the day at Rathna Ella to resume duties elsewhere. He had seen it all. He was neutral to human suffering.

7

It was a slow fall first. She had just pulled her daughter to safety. In the process she had started to slide down. First, she thought she could rebalance herself and stop the forward movement. She would have done it, had the rocks and pebbles not been so slippery. The big rocks were covered in slime and it was like trying to balance herself on ice. She had watched ice skating and ballet on ice. But that would have taken endless hours of practice. Here she was, a middle-aged house wife, trying to fight against gravity and friction or rather, the lack of it. She had no chance. When she tried to step on the smaller pebbles, they just rolled on, taking her feet with her.

She reached out in desperation and in fact managed to catch hold of some grass with her left hand. But they were plants with shallow roots in wet land. They just came in her hand. Before she knew it, she was at the edge. She knew this was the end. She had no chance. Her last thoughts were about her two children.

She was expecting a crack followed by excruciating pain. Then the water would consume her. Is this how it would have felt for the recent air crash victims who went down in sea? Her entire life played out in her head, in fast forward mode. Her dead mother's face loomed in the background. I am coming home mama thought Lakshmy.

It was long and slow. The expected thud never came. The pain was not there! It was like she was on a water slide. Is something holding her? Why is she floating in air? Is she in water or air? She certainly had water in front of her. She was actually behind the falls, in front of the rock. This was surreal. She was surrounded by water but she did not have any problems breathing. It was like a slow motion fall.

She was not sure what was happening. It was as if she was being held by a supernatural force to break the impact of the fall. The water falling in front of her was moving faster than she was. How was that possible? It was perplexing. Had she already died? She had heard that once death envelops you there would be no pain. No suffering. All the sufferings are inflicted by the body it takes. The soul is pristine, unblemished and blissful, she had been taught. So had she left her body? Had she died? Was she just thin ether? Why then did she have awareness, consciousness and ability to think? She was confused. If she had died, what happens next? Where were the dead relatives? Was this all just tricks played by her brain due to lack of oxygen? Was she drowning?

It felt like an eternity. Then she felt her feet touch the rock beneath. Her feet had landed. In fact it was the left foot first and then the right. They had been moving in a cyclical motion as though she was on a paddleboat. This happened without any thought and certainly, there was no planning on her part. Suddenly she realised that she would fall forward on impact. What happened in reality was just the opposite. She fell backwards. Oh her head! She thought she was going to bang her head against the rock face. She didn't! It was as though some one had held her gently laid her on the bedrock. She should have fallen headfirst but here she was landing on her feet softly. She should have fallen forward. She had fallen on her back. She should have crashed hard on the rock. She had a soft landing. She should have been dead. She was still alive. She thought there was just the rock pool at the bottom but here she was, lying between the rock at the back and the waterfall in front. She should have drowned but she didn't. The whole event should have been over in an instant but it had lasted an aeon. It was as though she was trapped in a time machine; in a place where time stood still; where the past, present and future merged. Everything condensed into the eternal moment of NOW! She was in that supranormal state of consciousness. Was this what the Buddhists call Nirvana? Was this what the Hindus call Mukthi? Or was this what the Abrahamic religions call Heaven? Well how long had she been in that state? She of course had lost the concept of time. Time matter and energy were interchangeable and had no meaning at that point for her.

Then she fainted. At least she lost her consciousness as humans understood. She lost the ability to think, reason, or feel. She must have passed out.

When Lakshmy regained consciousness, she was floating in water. She was lying on a circular object. Was it a raft or a dinghy? She had no idea. She was being gently rocked in the water. There was no waterfall. She was in a lake. The waves were soothing and the wind whistled softly. She felt like Mother Nature was singing lullaby. Where was she? What was she lying on? Why was she not panicking? The object she was lying on was circular with numerous firm radially arranged spokes emanating from a central axle. Yes it was a wheel. A wheel like no other she had seen. Though there were gaps between the 'spokes' water did not seep in. For an object that felt solid, it was strangely buoyant.

The sun was setting. Sunset in this lake was a sight to behold. Or was it sun rise? Was it the same day or the next? Lakshmy did not feel afraid at all. She was sure she was in the land of the living. She was sure she had survived. She was also sure help would arrive soon. It was as though some strange power had taken her over into its protection. Why should she worry? If she had been protected from the devastating fall in Rathna Ella, why should she be worried about drowning in this lake? Then she saw some small fishing boats coming towards her. She had survived!

8

They had searched everywhere along the Hasalaka river. It was to no avail. The divers to look in the bottom rock pool could come only after daybreak due to logistical reasons. The villagers and the police had looked at the entire Hasalaka River downstream from the falls. Yet there was no sign of Lakshmy. With nightfall, they had to suspend the search. The children were crying all the time, asking for their mother. Sunil and Fernando continued the search on their own even through the night, with the help of lanterns. They were hoping for some clues. At least if they could retrieve the body there would be some closure. Otherwise, the question of what happened to Lakshmy would linger on throughout their lives.

They left the children with some kind village women who, even though they did not know English, could still communicate. Compassion and humanity don't have a language do they? But how could they comfort two young children who had suddenly lost their mother?

That was the longest night they had ever endured. It was painful. Their minds were numb with grief. None had slept even a second. Will this darkness ever end?

That was when a villager came running. They had spotted a woman on a boat like object, floating in Hasalaka Lake. They were not sure if she was alive or not. There had been movements but that could be due to the sway of the boat in the waves. She was spotted at daybreak, at first light. They were not sure how long she had been there. She could have been floating in the lake all night. They had no way to tell. Certainly, there had been no one in that area when the last fishermen moored their boats and left the previous night.

Soon the boats went racing towards the middle of the lake. Sunil was taken to the lakeshore. es it was Lakshmy! And she was alive! Not only alive she was also very well! It was as if she was waking up from slumber. What a miracle! The lake was upstream from the waterfalls where she was swept away. How did she end up in the lake? Surely, the water currents should have taken her in the opposite direction!

What was the object she was floating on? Was it a wheel of a big vehicle? It was certainly not a boat. It had gaps between the slender tubes that served as spokes. There were millions of tiny holes in those tubes too. Why isn't water getting into this contraption? It was all very strange.

For the children the fact that their mother was alive was all that mattered. They did not care about how she ended up where she was. They would take her as she was, no matter what. Sunil too did not want to think about the science and logic behind her mysterious disappearance and reappearance. He was overjoyed to see Lakshmy alive.

For Mr Fernando this was a big relief. He may not retire after all. Except for the previous day, his job had been the most enjoyable thing he did in his life. Perhaps he would continue. He knew things did not add up. Strange things kept happening repeatedly on this tour. Until yesterday, they were intriguing.

Yesterday was scary and frightful. If it continued to be like that, he could not take it. However, he thought, whatever power that was playing with their lives did not want to harm them. In fact, it had saved them. Looking at it another way, it saved them from the snake the other day, and it saved Lakshmy from the falls yesterday. So why not submit to the power and enjoy the ride?

Lakshmy could not remember many details. She remembered trying to snatch Kavitha from the edge of the water. That was all she could remember. Then she found herself floating in the lake. She was not shaken or traumatised. She was not even afraid of the water.

The family all huddled together in a group hug. All of them cried, including Sunil the Kargil veteran. They were tears of joy and relief not tears of sorrow or fear.

The villagers organised a celebratory feast. They made Kiribath (milk rice) and hoppers in honour of the tourist family that had endeared themselves to this place. They were also thankful to Lord Buddha for saving this young woman, and most of all saving the mother for the two children. The Mishras too cancelled all their programmes for the day. They were just happy to be together and happy that they were amidst such hospitable and caring people.

Lakshmy wanted the floating wheel to be taken back to India with her. She was going to take it as a lucky charm. She was going to enshrine it in her house in honour of her second coming. Sunil chided her for taking this junk back with her. "It is not junk my dear!

It saved my life!" Lakshmy was even willing to forego some of the space set aside for her saree shopping.

"Don't worry my dear. I will make sure all your collections are sent back one way or another." Mr Fernando was happy to help. He was willing to ensure that all the memorabilia from this wonderful trip would go back with the family. They deserved it, as this was turning out to be a magical holiday. This was turning out to be the most interesting of all the trips where he had been the guide.

The incident at the waterfall did not dampen the spirits as much as it would have if Lakshmy had been physically injured or psychologically scarred. Instead, she had emerged with a new glow and a lot more energy than she had previously. She was keen to continue with their original plans, though delayed by a day.

The next day it was a trip to Dambana. Dambana was a village where Veddhas lived. Veddhas are indigenous people of Sri Lanka. Legend has it that they are descendants of Yakkas. In common parlance the word Yakka meant demons but it probably derived from the name for the indigenous ethnic group that was considered uncivilised or wild. According to Mahavamsa, the ancient chronicle, Vijaya and his friends came from North-east India by boat. Vijaya befriended the Yakka princess Kuveni, married her, and then left her to marry a Pandyan princess from South India. The main ethnic group, the Sinhalese believe they are descendants of this alliance. They also believe that Vijaya had two children with Kuveni, who were banished into wilderness and who then inhabited and populated the area in Western Sri Lanka around Adams Peak. These are the people referred to as Veddhas, some believe. The province that contains the famous Adams Peak Mountain is called Sabbaragamuwa, which translates as the place of wild men.

Whether these beliefs are true or not is anybody's guess. It is common for people to associate myths and stories about their origins in their quest to find relevance. The arrival by boat is a theme that is also believed by Maoris of New Zealand who believe they came in canoes from a land called Hawaiki (not Hawaii). People in Christchurch in New Zealand still associate themselves with the names of the original immigrant ships that took them from Britain. Other immigrant nations too try to trace their origins. Many Australians are proud of their convict origins. Recently many African Americans are tracing their origins to the African nations. The yearning to trace one's roots is common among all cultures.

The other common thread in these origins stories is the attribution of one ethnic group to one particular ancestor who was a brother or stepbrother of the father of another ethnic group. Even in the Book of Genesis, the Jews are mentioned as being descendants of Abraham's second son Isaac, Abraham's eldest son Ishmael is believed to have been the patriarch of many prominent Arab tribes. In other words, the authors of such books have tried to find a common thread between races and portray them as distant cousins. Whether anthropology can be expressed in such simple terms is an open question.

Be it what it may have been, it is a fact that Yakkas or indigenous people existed before the current predominant races inhabited the island. Some believe Yakkas to be Ravana's people. With the passage of time, most were assimilated into the predominant cultures of the land, Tamil and Sinhala. The Veddah language is now spoken only in the area around Dambana, with the others taking up the above two languages. Even the surviving Veddah language has borrowed freely from Sinhala and Tamil to supplement its limited lexicon.

Concentrations of Veddhas lived in and around Dambana, Bintenne in Badulla district and around the ancient capital city of Anuradhapura. Most have been Sinhalised. The east coast Veddahs live in the Eastern Batticaloa and Trincomalee districts and have been living as Tamils. Lord Murugan (Subramanian)'s second consort, Valli is supposed to be a Veddah damsel. Veddah traditions are intricately intertwined with the worship of Murugan in Kathirgamam (Kataragama) and Uganthai in the Southeast corner of the island. Some of these traditions are even followed in Sella Sannithi, another famous shrine for Murugan in the Northern Jaffna peninsula.

The Veddahs follow a mixture of animism, Buddhism and Hinduism. They worship dead ancestors. As far as Mr Fernando was aware, they did not worship Ravana. Did they consider themselves descendants of Ravana? The mystical traditions of the land all merge and it is hard to differentiate one from the other.

When they reached there, it was mid-morning. The Veddahs were clad in loincloth or minimal attire. They were dark skinned and longhaired. They did not have much body hair. The women stayed in the background. They were hunter-gatherers and meat eaters. They hunted with bow and arrow. They had axes too. They kept moving in the jungle. They did do migrant swidden cultivation – they would clear one area of the jungle, burn the trees and plant their crops. They would then move to another area for the next season. This was similar to what some of the aboriginal tribes did in Australia and the natives did in South America. This way the fertility of the land is maintained over a long period. There was communal living and sharing.

They also had specific meat preserving techniques. They used honey collected from jungles to preserve meat. This ensured a continuous supply of meat throughout the year. Though their cousins in the East coast also did fishing, the tribe that the Mishras visited did not. They were mainly hunters.

They lived in thatched huts. Their habitat has been gradually eroded by modernization and development. The various irrigation and colonization schemes of successive governments have ensured the progressive shrinking of the hunting ground. On top of that, there were also wild life rules etc. that protected some species.

With tourist arrivals being another source of income their lifestyles were changing rapidly. They were very hospitable and entertained the family with their variety of food. They were friendly. The family was treated to a sumptuous meal of roasted Kabaragoya, a variety of monitor. They also had venison. The meat tasted salty but was soft. While Sunil ate everything, Lakshmy and the children refused to eat the lizard.

The children had never seen indigenous people. They had heard about Nilgiris and the native people there. Sunil had visited Andaman Islands during the course of his work. Lakshmy the teacher did not miss the opportunity to inculcate in the children the respect for other cultures, however primitive they may seem to us. We have no right to judge. In fact, many of the belief systems of indigenous people including animism may be closer to the truth than what many religions teach, she said.

They stayed the night at Dambana. That night they had a special dance. It was the incantation of the ancestors. Young men clad in loincloth carrying twigs in their hands danced around a fire, to the beating drums. These drums were different to the Thovil drums. The dancing involved vigorous movements of the torso as well as the legs. The arms carrying the twigs swayed in tune with the rhythmic body movements.

While the whole community was gathered around the fire, the visitors too were provided with seats. An old woman was chanting the incantations. She appeared to be in a trance. She was old with matted grey hair, which was somewhat unkempt. She was topless with drooping breasts. She wore a lungi to cover her modesty. She was alternatively standing and squatting. After about an hour, she started dancing with the men. Suddenly she started going around the fire in circular movements. Then she came towards Lakshmy. Dancing around for a few minutes, she zeroed in on Lakshmy. Lakshmy was scared and surprised. The old woman beckoned Lakshmy to get up. She then held Lakshmy's hands firmly. Though her grip was firm, it was not crushing or threatening. He looked into Lakshmy's eyes. Her eyes were blood shot. It was as if she was trying to look through Lakshmy and beyond, at a distance behind her. All the while, she was continuing the chanting. Then she paused for a moment. After that, she started to speak.

She was speaking in a trance. She spoke in Sinhala first and then started in English! Yes she started speaking English in a typical Indian accent, rolling the 'R's and dragging the vowels. She said, "Ravana Rajah is asking take that wheel with you. He is helping you! He wants to help Sita's people"

Lakshmy was flabbergasted. Firstly, how did this Veddah woman know English? Then how can she speak in the same accent as I do? Even if that is a setup, how did she know about the wheel? No one present here except her own family and Mr Fernando knew about the wheel and the events at Rathna Falls.

If she did not believe that Ravana's spirit was following them before, she certainly believed it now. She was not scared any more. She knew that the spirit was actually helping them and will not harm them, Sita's people.

The woman relaxed her grip. She gently patted Lakshmy on her cheeks, and said in English "Go to Kataragama. There is a great seer there who will have answers to your questions."

Having said this, the lady appeared to faint. The others were expecting this, and quickly lay her on the ground and splashed water on her face. They had seen it before. Usually the woman would go into a different state and then faint. When she woke up, she wouldn't remember anything.

When she came to Lakshmy tried to talk to her in English. This woman did not tell me whom I should meet in Kataragama. Perhaps she can be clearer thought Lakshmy. When she accosted her and started asking questions the old woman was puzzled. She did not understand why this foreigner was talking to her. Nor did she understand a word of the language she was speaking in. She smiled at Lakshmy sheepishly. Obviously, she had forgotten what had transpired just a little while ago.

When they retired for the night, the children cried. Both Ajay and Kavitha had had enough. They had been haunted by strange happenings all through this trip. It culminated in the episode where their mother went missing for nearly a whole day, where they thought she had died. Now this old woman is telling their mother strange things about Ravana and Sita. They couldn't take it anymore.

"I want to go home!" cried Kavitha. This was becoming emotionally draining. They were not enjoying the trip anymore.

"I can't wait to go too," Ajay chimed in. The children seldom agreed on anything. But today they were united. Tears were welling up in both their eyes.

"Beta and Beti, let's just go to Katharagama. After that, we will go home. Having come all this way we don't want to miss out on Lord Karthikeya," Sunil was proposing a compromise. Actually, they were going to spend some time in the Yala wild life park and spend a few days in the Northern Jaffna peninsula where Sunil had a distant relative through marriage. All that can go but he did not want to miss out on Kataragama, especially after what the lady had said in her trance. He did not want to leave with unfinished business. If Ravana was trying to tell them something, they should give him a chance to do that. If they cut short their trip now they would never know what he was trying to tell, nor would they find out the significance of the pieces of equipment or remnants of it that they were regularly chancing upon. Surely, this can't all be co incidental. If the theme 'helping Sita's people' was recurring, what was its significance? Who are Sita's people? Does it mean Indian people? In that case, will the information he is trying to convey benefit his country? If that was the case, he certainly did not want to stop this process half way.

Mr Fernando also placated the children. He said Kataragama, or Kathirgamam in Tamil, is a once in a lifetime experience. Having come all this was they should not miss this experience.

That sealed the deal. They would spend a day lazing around in Mahiyangana and then make their way to Kataragama they decided.

9

Kathirgamam or Kataragama is an ancient shrine venerated equally by Hindus and Buddhists as well as Sufi Muslims. However, it originated as a Veddah place of worship for their hunting god, Kande Yakka. They worshipped in a thatched mud hut, with a spear planted upright representing the god. Soon the Tamils incorporated this into their worship of Kandan or Subramanian or Kartikeya, the warlord. There are several theories about the origin of Kandan worship. Iskander was the name by which Alexander the great was known in Persia. Even before that, there is evidence that Kartikeya was worshipped in Indus valley civilization.

Kande Yakka and Kandan became one and the same. His second consort Valli hailed from a Veddah clan in Kathirgamam. In the meantime, he was incorporated into Buddhist worship as Kataragama Deiyyo. In Sri Lanka where the predominant strain of Buddhism is the non-theistic Theravada, worship of many Hindu Gods as Bodhisattvas is common. The worship of Kataragama Deiyyo has been around for at least 1500 years. Another difference of this temple to the mainstream Hindu temples is that the main sanctum sanctorum of the presiding Deity is always covered by a curtain. The priest does the poojas inside while the devotees wait in the outer precincts. It is believed that if a layperson tries to look inside, he will be destroyed by one calamity or another. Furthermore, there is no chanting of Mantras – some priests even wear a gag mask over their mouths. The poojas are done in silence while the drums, bells etc. make noises outside. The main shrine is serviced by priests who descended from Veddah clans and who are not Brahmins. Some may eat meat. Another distinct feature are the drums – they are not the regular thavil or mritangam which are the percussion instruments of choice in mainstream South Indian or Sri Lankan Hindu festivals and temples. These are drums called parai and belong to a class of drums played at funerals. Thus, the rituals have distinctive features reflecting their Veddah origins. There are a series of Murugan temples in Sri Lanka that have these features. Uhanthai Murugan temple in Okantha and Sella Sannithi temple in Jaffna are examples.

The rituals related to Veddah traditions are limited to the main Murugan Temple and the Valli Amman temple. The separate Deivanai Amman temple and Ganesh temple are in the lines of traditional Hindu temples both in structure and in rituals.

Even Sufi Muslims venerate the shrine and have their own myths about it in relation to Prophet Mohammed and so on. Sufism is a fringe religious faction in Sri Lanka. The majority are Sunni Muslims. Though mystical Islam was reasonably popular in the Eastern towns such as Kattankudi, the spread of Salafism through scholarships and funding primarily from Saudi has eroded into these atypical varieties of Islam. Nevertheless, Kataragama harbours the tomb of a famous Islamic saint.

Such a place of importance to three religions and all ethnic groups in Sri Lanka attracts millions of people every year. The main festival occurs in July.

Fortunately for the Mishras, they happened to be visiting at the correct time.

It was afternoon when they reached the temple. The actual temple complex has been kept simple. Except for a coating of bright yellow (what a taste) on the outer wall, not much has been altered. The feared God is not to be tampered with. However, the other temples have had adornments and expansion. There was a large Buddhist temple called Kiri Vihara in the vicinity. This is milky white. Though the main temple has remained the same, the facilities for pilgrims have expanded exponentially. The Ramakrishna Mutt has had a long presence in the area and provided simple but clean accommodation. There are many new restrooms and hotels that have sprung up recently. The roads have been expanded and upgraded. There used to be a time when people had to go by narrow jungle routes on bullock carts.

Though the access was easy, it also brought new hazards. Improved roads meant more road accidents. Mr Fernando filled them with awe of the feared God of war with many stories where people with unfulfilled vows or those who indulged in activities unbecoming of a holy place met with untimely deaths on their way to or from the shrine. There were stories of entire families being wiped out when their vehicles rolled over enroute to the temple city.

Mr Fernando said, "Don't mess with Kataragama Deiyyo. If you can't keep a vow in a timely fashion don't vow to him. He will always keep a count!"

"Well the safest is not to vow anything," said Lakshmy. "At least Ravana was protective. This God is serious business it looks like!"

Another hazard was the snakes. Again, if you are not in the good books of this God he is not going to protect you from these creatures. It must have been scary for the people who went from Jaffna to Kathirgamam on foot those days. This tradition continues to this day. The facilities are better now. The main part of the deal is if you say you will do something, do it. Don't take chances with Kataragama.

If Lakshmy was going to ask Him to protect them from Ravana before, she thought better of it now. She did not want to complicate matters by involving two super natural forces in this. It may start a celestial war. When the Gods fight, it is man who suffers.

Having a healthy respect for the presiding deity, they decided to worship and take part in the ceremonies recommended by Mr Fernando. Then they would finish this holiday and get back home. The children were already yearning for home food. Tasty as it is, Sri Lankan food is generally hotter and Sri Lankans used different oils than those used in their home food.

Their first port of call was Sella Kathirgamam temple. This was situated away from the main temple complex. The Manikka Ganga wound its way around the whole area. The temple was by the river. It was rumoured that there were gemstones among the pebbles of this sacred river. There were certainly many rocks and stones through which the river weaved. Whether there were gems or not there certainly were many fish. In fact, there were thousands of fish, which seemed unperturbed by the presence of bathers. The latter did not harm them in this sacred place. The fish in fact nibbled and nestled their way around the feet of the people. Both Kavitha and Ajay were thrilled at having a river bath in such idyllic settings. Lakshmy too seemed to have overcome the trauma of the fall at the waterfall. She too revelled in the waters.

Having first been to the Ganesh temple, they could now spend the rest of the day at the main complex. That night Mr Fernando had arranged for them to watch fire walking. This was another phenomenon that was believed to have paranormal connotations. Lakshmy was certain that Ravana would make contact in the night. She was excited and worried at the same time. Were they being held hostage by some ancient spirit? What is he trying to achieve?

It was late at night that the fire walking started. A large area was cleared and viewing stands had been erected around the central rectangular arena where all the activity was. In the middle, a pyre of wood was set alight. The smoke and incense were making people dizzy and their eyes were tearing. Some coughed and some found breathing difficult. But the people waited with patience. The drumbeats were creating an atmosphere of mystical expectations. This time the drums were of conventional thavil type and were accompanied by nadhaswaram, the South Indian wind instrument. People were dancing, and chanting "arohara" intermittently. Bells were ringing. The light emanating from the burning wood was far brighter than the light from the tube lights tied to the posts.

Once the burning wood became embers this was spread into a rectangular pit in the centre. The firewalkers lined up on one side. Many were clad in saffron dhotis while others wore white. Most were men but there were some women too. All had prayed at the temple and wore the holy ash and kunkum or sandan thilaks on their foreheads. There was religious fervour everywhere. On one side there were people who had their bodies pierced by small metal lances as penance to Lord Murugan. The piercing of tongue and lips appeared particularly painful to the onlookers. Some were carrying kavadis the ornately decorated cross bar structure carried on the shoulders. These had to be balanced while they danced.

Then someone who appeared to be the MC broke a coconut to start the proceedings. One by one, the firewalkers walked the walk. Some ran, some hopped and others walked leisurely. Volunteers applied paraffin to their feet. None appeared to be in pain.

How can this be possible? The worship of Murugan has been associated with many masochistic rituals from ancient days. Some roll around the sand covered outer precincts of temples bare cheated, bearing the pain from the numerous cuts and abrasions. Some pierce their bodies while some carry burdens called kavadis. One rare form of this is called thooku kavadi where the practitioner is suspended from a height by hooks that pierce the skin on the back.

This self-deprival is not confined to Hinduism. Other religions too practice fasting, flogging and crucifixion. The aspirants do not seem to feel the pain. The believers think this is due to divine intervention but many rationalists have tried to have a scientific explanation. Dr Carlo Fonseka and Dr Abraham Kovoor have tried to debunk these by doing fire walking themselves in the sixties. Various theories have been put forward including the thickened epidermis in people who walk barefooted normally in their daily lives, minimising contact time to any one part of the foot when they walk fast or run, and the release of endorphins, the natural painkillers.

The rationalist movement made news in the sixties and seventies. Then the war took over. For thirty years, Sri Lankans' main worry was the war and war alone. The war brought misery. In this misery thrived the various religious groups including many neo Christian evangelicals. So the rationalists just dispersed. They could not hold the attention of the public anymore.

Fire walking continues to induce fear and faith in the Sri Lankan people. It is not confined to Kathirgamam and it is not restricted to Murugan temples. Many Kali temples have this ritual in their festivals. The Pattini Amman temple in Western Sri Lanka is another famous site for this particular ritual.

The highlight for the children was the fire eating show put on by some of the participants. They seemed to be able to put out flames of burning torches by their mouths. It was really amazing that they did not get burnt.

"How do they do that dad?" asked Ajay.

"I don't know beta. I have seen people do flaming shots in the West!" said Sunil. Surely, there must be a trick to this.

"I know for sure that they don't coat their mouths with anything prior to this." Fernando must have read his mind. He preferred to believe this to be another of the phenomena we don't understand. Not everything can be explained by science. Nor does it need to be. It is sometimes better to soak up the atmosphere and enjoy the moment than to try to think rationally.

"Ravana hasn't turned up today." said Lakshmy with a bit of disappointment showing in her voice.

"Let the bugger have a day off Lakshmy" said Sunil. Maybe the spirit of Ravana was their figment of imagination. Perhaps there was nothing to their recent experiences.

"Does that mean you can extend your holidays?" asked Fernando. He wanted people to enjoy his beautiful motherland for as long as possible.

"We want to go home," said the children. That settled the issue.

They slept well, not having to think of the strange events that had occurred in the last few days. The next morning was going to be an arduous hill climb.

Early to bed children, said Lakshmy, giving Sunil some hope for the night. Well it was early by the Sri Lankan standards as it was already past 10 'clock when they returned to their accommodation. Lakshmy politely declined. "This is a sacred city. Let's be vegetarian."

It was early start the next day. The task was to climb a hill called Kathiramalai. It was also known as Wedihitikande in Sinhala. There was a temple in mid-level and a Buddhist temple at the top. The mountain was only some 300 meters high, being a poor cousin to the high mountains of the middle of the country. The mountain is steeped in history and spirituality.

The low-lying forest on the mountain was different to the wetlands of Hasalaka. The soil was dry with a hue of reddish brown. The trees were shorter. The greenery was darker. As they climbed the steps, the vista before them unfolded in breath taking colours. The experience was worthwhile just for the scenery if not for the spirituality. In any case, what spirituality can a couple with two children seek on a trip like this? They did visit the Hindu temple and the Buddhist shrine at the summit.

There was an elderly monk at the Buddhist temple. The temple had parts, which were built probably more than 2000 years ago according to local legend. The stupa itself was a simple structure compared to the larger shrines in Polonnoruwa. It was white and was bell shaped. The monk accosted Sunil. He said "Sadhu sadhu." By now, Sunil was well versed in greeting Buddhist monks.

"Ravana Rajah has sent you here," the elder said. "I can sense the vibes around you. You seem very special."

The family was perplexed. Just when they thought they had gotten over the Ravana madness, here they go again! This was not funny anymore.

"Why are you saying this venerable monk?" asked Sunil.

"Don't ignore me. Ravana's spirit has roamed our land ever since he was killed, aeons ago. It would appear that it is seeking to fulfil an unfulfilled obligation or duty before it attains peace. It has chosen you as the vehicle. I don't know much beyond this. If you want to know more, you need to seek the help of an anjanam practitioner. They will be able to garner more information. In fact, there is one such person at the base of this hill. His name is Sumanatissa. I know for a fact that Ravana's spirit talks to him from time to time. He has helped people track down the criminals in many major murders and robberies over the years."

Saying this he blessed them and tied pirith noola around the wrists of all of them. The practice of tying these charmed strings around the wrists is very common among Hindus and Buddhists in Sri Lanka.

Ok, this trip was ending soon. Before that, they wanted to find out why Ravana was haunting them. In any case, they would be rid of him as soon as they landed in India. He wouldn't dare to come to India again. Last time he went to India he got into major trouble, ending up abducting Mrs Rama and eventually losing almost his entire family in the ensuing battle. So let us indulge him for the day. That was Sunil's rationale when he convinced his family to accompany him to meet the mystic. Mr Fernando was flexible. They had parked at the base of the hill. They decided to descend by the circular road rather than the steps. This way they were able to find the hut as described by the monk.

When they knocked on the door there was no answer for a long time. The door was closed but not locked. After about 10 minutes of trying knocking and calling out, Sunil opened the door. The inside had two rooms only. The connecting doorway did not have a door. The elevated sill at the bottom was wooden, as was the frame. There was a curtain, which was barely covering half the area. Since there was no one in the outer room, Sunil and Fernando carefully stepped in and peeped through the doorway to perp inside the inner room. They made sure they had removed their footwear, as was customary in Sri Lankan homes.

Inside the second room a man was seated cross-legged on the floor in Padmasana, meditating. He was old, with a big white moustache and a long white beard. He wore an orange dhoti but was bare chested. His eyes were closed. He had matted white hair, which had been braided in Rastafarian style and tied above his head in a bun. He wore a kunkum thilak in the middle of his holy ash covered forehead.

As they entered, he opened his eyes. Staring at them, he said in Sinhala "Don't you know I am meditating? I don't see anyone till after 5 o' clock!"

Mr Fernando profusely apologised. He pleaded that they were from outside the area and that the guests were in fact from India. This only caused the hermit to raise his brows in a questioning expression. Then

Fernando said the Buddhist priest sent them from the summit temple. The moment he heard this, the man's facial expression mellowed and he broke out in a smile. "Oh you were sent by Swami? Ok what can I do for you? Are you alone?"

He quickly invited Lakshmy and the children in. They only had bare furniture in this hut. A cot made of rope and a couple of low benches. The visitors were thankful they could sit, having climbed the mountain all day, their legs were tired.

"What do you want from me?" asked the ascetic. Mr Fernando explained the reason. He told the man how they had been followed by what they believed was Ravana's spirit. How strange things were happening to them and how they ended up chancing upon these objects, which looked very different to what they had ever seen in their lives.

The man thought for a while. He said, "I used to do clairvoyance previously but I have given up those black magic techniques. I am concentrating on the real things that will uplift my soul." Saying this he looked intently at Lakshmy. He asked, "You have the name of Mahalakshmy! Do you know Sita Devi was an Avatar of Mahalakshmy?"

They all wondered how he got her name correct. He then said, "Where have you kept the wheel?"

Again, they had told him they found strange objects but they hadn't told him one of the objects was a wheel. In this strange world of clairvoyance, nothing should surprise them.

Mr Fernando offered to go to the room and collect the wheel but the ascetic said, "Why don't you all go, have lunch and come at 5 pm."

They went off, having made an appointment with destiny for 5 o'clock. They were excited at the possibility of knowing more about this spirit that appeared to follow them. They also had a sense of foreboding as to what this would bring upon their family. Especially Lakshmy was worried. She thought she might lose Sunil as a result of what he was going to tell them. Though they tried to have an afternoon nap, none of them could sleep.

The appointed time came. They were back at the mystic's hut. This time he had spread a large mat in the inner room. The visitors all sat cross-legged on the mat. The wheel was placed in front of the clients. The clairvoyant sat facing them, cross-legged on a small mat with the wheel placed between them. He lit a lamp with camphor, said some incantations and broke a coconut. He then burnt some twigs and incense on a small clay hearth. Chanting some mantras repeatedly he invoked the blessings of Murugan first and then Kali. This went on for more than half an hour. He then invited Ravana to attend. The room was filled with smoke. They could hardly see each other or anything else in the room. The sun had gone down and the only light in the room was from the lamp and the burning fire in the middle. The flames had subsided and it was only ash and ember by now, emitting black smoke. Then the ascetic collected some of the burnt ash and mixed it with water, making a thick paste. He then drew some figures using this paste applied on his right index finger, on a betel leaf. He seemed to be in a trance and his voice became louder and louder. It reached a crescendo and stopped.

We should have kept the children out of this thought Lakshmy. She was getting really scared. She had heard stories about black magic gone wrong. Suppose he makes a slight mistake and invokes another ghost, say Ramanna instead of Ravana and this earlier ghost is a criminal? This ghost may then follow them everywhere. She shuddered to think. The ghost could turn amorous or it could even be a paedophile! Lakshmy thought why did I come here in the first place and why did I bring the children?

The clairvoyant was oblivious to all these doubts in her mind. He knew his game well. After stopping for a second or two, he started speaking in a different tone in a different dialect and much louder than before. It sounded like a mixture of Hindi and Tamil. However, they could not understand anything.

Presently the man started a conversation with himself. It was like Kramer versus Kramer. He would talk in his normal voice for a while and then would switch to this strange language in the other voice. This went on for a little while. Then the ascetic rang a bell, snuffed the lamp out and put out the fire. He did have electricity and he switched the lights on in the room.

He was quiet for a little while, probably recovering from the high he had been on. Then he spoke slowly in Sinhala. Mr Fernando was the translator.

He said reverentially "You have been lucky to have caught the attention of Ravana Rajah. He met his untimely death aeons ago at the hands of Rama. He has felt remorse for kidnapping someone else's wife and imprisoning her for many years. He has been roaming this landscape not knowing how to get rid of this guilt. He thinks that by helping Sita's people he can redress the grave wrong he had done her. When he saw Sunil and Lakshmy he thought that they could be the vehicle through which he could do his penance and achieve his solace.

"The people of Bharat are the rightful heirs of Sita. He wants to help Bharat achieve great glory. The parts that you have been finding, or rather he has been helping you to find, are from his Pushpaka Vimana. His flying chariot had far more advanced technology than is known to the current civilization. He wants you to take these with you, analyse them and find ways to improve the efficiency and capabilities of the flying machines in your air force.

"He has given you the clues. It is up to you to find ways to use this technology. If you don't make use of this, then it is not his problem. Having said this he disappeared. He will not trouble you again unless you want him."

Having said this, the ascetic fell into a state of deep slumber. May be he was exhausted. May be he was in meditation. The family was afraid to move. Mr Fernando indicated that the man might have more revelations. They waited.

Suddenly he opened his eyes. "Did I tell you this? He said that the Pushpaka Vimana was shot down. He knows only the parts that fell in certain places. The engine was actually taken by Hanuman and was hidden in a mountain cave. He doesn't know the exact location. But he knows where you can obtain the information."

"How can we find out?" asked Sunil.

"After killing Ravana, Rama was inflicted with Brahma Hathi Dosha, as Ravana was a Brahmin from his father's side. In order to be rid of this, Rama worshipped Lord Shiva in Rameshwaram. There he confessed his killing to the priest. He also gave details of where the engine is hidden. This information is passed from generation to generation. The father tells the son at the time of ordination into priesthood about the great yanthra that is hidden. They are told to await the man who will come looking for this information. Generation after generation has perished without the arrival of this messiah, with the truth buried deep in their hearts. The events were so distant that nowadays they just include this piece of information as part of the rite of passage without knowing the real meaning of this. In fact, a mantra that will unlock the secret is also incorporated in the pooja ritual.

"And if you are thinking it was passed to the main priests at the Rameshwaram temple you are wrong. The lucky line of priests tends to a small Shiva temple near Mandothari's sea in Danushkodi. You need to seek him out and tell him that you are Ravana's messenger looking for the yanthra. Saying this he beckoned Sunil. He whispered a mantra in his ear. "The priest will ask you for a password and this mantra will serve as the password. Good luck to you."

Sunil was not supposed to divulge this mantra to anyone, not even Lakshmy. Well Lakshmy demanded to know the mantra but Sunil refused to tell her. This led to an argument that night. "You never trust me with secrets," cried Lakshmy. It was the same story about his work. He knew a lot of classified information, which he was under oath not to reveal anyone. Every now and then Lakshmy would probe, only to hit a brick wall. "When we married we promised to each other that we will never hold back anything between us," was her angst. She could never understand how a husband could hold secrets from his wife, even if they are work related. This will be a bone of contention till he retired probably.

With that, they decided to end the Sri Lankan holiday. It had been an unusual one and it had left Sunil with work to do. The two metal objects had been sent with Radhika as arranged with Fernando. Lakshmy was under the impression that they were sent as unaccompanied baggage. Neither Fernando nor Sunil wanted another flare up by saying Radhika took them. As for the wheel, Lakshmy was fond of it as it saved her life. She was happy to take it with her. As they had cut short the holidays there was no time for much shopping anyway. Mr Fernando used his contacts with the customs and security so that no one questioned what that strange looking object was at this end.

10

It had been a couple of months since his return from Sri Lanka. Sunil was assigned to the air force technical college in the Defence Forces Colony. They lived in the colony. The work involved very little commute. The children had settled into their school routine. Bangalore is a beautiful city. In spite of the recent massive expansion and modernisation, some parts have retained the old colonial charm. The DFC area was one of them. With large trees lining the streets and spacious parks dotting the area, the old British buildings with tall ceilings were a blast from the past. When you are living in such ethereal surroundings, you don't normally appreciate how lucky you are. With the mundane tasks of work and family life occupying his time, days were passing very fast. He had completely forgotten about the Sri Lankan holiday and the Ravana episode.

Not that Ravana had left them at the shores of Sri Lanka. Their passage back to India had been an ordeal. The customs officer had refused to allow the "wheel" without first demanding to know what it was. It took a lot of explaining and intervention of Sunil's seniors to make him allow Sunil to take it into the country. They had to waste several hours at the Kempegowda International Airport in Devanahalli, making several frantic phone calls.

Gone were the days when the airport security was as lax as the fibres of cheesecloth. Sunil had heard of instances where the person manning the metal detectors would demand and get bribes to allow people to pass through. India was now a proud nation.

The younger generation were confident and full of self-belief and self-respect. The customs officer was quietly confident in what he did and was politely insistent on doing his duty with diligence. Sunil was proud of his countrymen even though he was annoyed by the inconvenience.

Once they were back home, the wheel went into a corner of the garage. Both Lakshmy and Sunil were inundated with the tasks of running a family. They had no time for anything else. It is not infrequent that people make resolutions during vacations where they are inspired by the relaxed environment in the destination, only to forget all about that on return. From changes in diet through taking up Yoga, meditation or sport, all these holiday inspired decisions are relegated to the back burner when the burden of running a household and bringing bread to the table resumes. If someone had mentioned Ravana to Sunil he would have asked Ravana who? Well if that somebody was not Radhika, that is.

The fateful call came one afternoon, just before Sunil was about to pack up for the day. "Call for Group Captain Sunil Mishra," the voice at the intercom said. "Put it through," said Sunil, irate that this call should come at 4 o'clock when he was planning to go early. He had to pick up Ajay as Lakshmy had an appointment with her beautician. Kavitha had sports and her mother would pick her up afterwards. This was the good thing about settled life when everything was predictable. That was also the bad thing. Predictability breeds complacence. People get used to their comfort zones. They add to their waistline. Then they get a heart attack. They die. What did they achieve? They leave behind everything that they worked for. The house, the bank accounts and the lot.

Annoyed at getting a call Sunil was somewhat placated when the voice at the other end turned out to be a sweet female voice. "It's Radhika," said the voice.

"Which Radhika?" asked Sunil, trying to think.

"You must be having a lot of girlfriends yaar! How many Radhikas do you know?" The high-pitched voice became even higher pitched. How can he forget? They had met just two months before.

"Oh, that Radhika? Did you want Lakshmy's number?" Sunil was trying to get away as it was getting late for Ajay.

"No! I can't reveal this to Lakshmy!" she said in a husky voice.

"What is it? Why are you so secretive?" asked Sunil. Radhika had had marital trouble. Maybe she has had a complication in that front and needed confidential advice or support. But why is she talking to a man, who will never understand women's issues?

"Have you forgotten the metal junk you asked me to carry yaar?" Now it struck him. Fernando had arranged for Radhika to carry that back to India. Sunil did not know that Lakshmy was unaware of it. In fact, Lakshmy thought that he was sending them as unaccompanied baggage at that time. However, they had both long forgotten about it.

"Ok ok. I remember. What happened to that?" Sunil was interested though he was still hard pressed for time.

"You are so cool about it Sunil! You don't know the endless trouble I have had with it!" Radhika sounded exasperated. How can this man talk like this when I had done him a favour?

"Oh that was on a whim. I am sorry if you had trouble with that. But actually I don't need the metal junk!" Sunil had some thrill seeking mindset during the holiday. Now he was back in the cycle of life where these distractions are not needed. And he had to go soon. He won't hear the end of it from Lakshmy if he went late even by a minute. Already he was being reminded several times a day how he has neglected his family.

"Well I agreed to take it with my luggage. I had trouble at Sri Lankan end but thanks to Mr Fernando's friends, I was allowed to go. However, at this end they stopped me. They were sure that there is some contraband hidden in the metal. They treated me like they were dealing with a drug mule." She was almost crying.

"They detained the objects for further testing. Even my own children were looking at me like I was doing something illegal. I had to go back to the airport twice to get it released. I am sure they must have my name in a terror suspects' list somewhere."

"I am sorry." That was all Sunil could say. He was genuinely sorry. "Why didn't you call me earlier?"

"I thought you were still in Sri Lanka. Besides, I thought you would call me as soon as you returned. Mr Fernando made it known that this was very important for you. I am disappointed."

She was entitled to be aggrieved. Why did Sunil put her through all this if this was only some trivial pursuit that he would forget soon?

"I am really sorry," said Sunil. Where is it now?"

"They released it alright after about a week and after a lot of explanation. I had to use my imagination. I did not want to put you in trouble. You know you work for defence services. I did not want any black mark to go on your file."

True. Sunil knew that even if he was able to explain his way out he would have this hanging over his head for the rest of his career. He may be overlooked for promotions based on this.

"Thank you Radhika. I am very grateful for your kindness."

Sunil did not want her to feel he was rushing her, after all that he had made her go through.

"That's alright. You can make it up to me later. Listen I called you because I am moving house. I had left your stuff in the garage and forgotten about it. But now that I am single, I am downsizing. The children are going to a boarding school. I am moving to a small apartment in close proximity to the hospital. The parking is in a communal area. I can't leave this in there. I really have to get rid of it now." Radhika had a reason to call now.

"When do you want me to remove it? When are you moving?" Sunil had to find a solution.

Radhika was moving in two weeks. Sunil explained that he had to pick up Ajay. He would come the next day and sort it out. With that, he left work. Throughout his drive, he was thinking how he was going to get out of this. He did not want Lakshmy to know that he had gone behind her back. He could not take it home. He had to find a way to house this stuff within two weeks. He certainly did not want to throw it. Not after putting Radhika through all this trouble. He owed it to her to do something with this metal object.

11

The drive to Ulsoor was not too bad. He had taken early leave from his work. He still hadn't figured out what he would do with Ravana's objects. He could leave it in his garage along with the wheel. He did not want Lakshmy to see them. Nor did he want her to know he was visiting Radhika. He will have a lot of explanation to do. He would rather not go through a series of interrogations. They say if you tell one lie, you will need to tell a hundred lies to cover that original sin. He could come clean and explain everything up front. He knew better. He did not want to hear the incriminations for the rest of his life. Or rather, add another to the list of reasons why he was not a good husband.

He would leave it in his car boot until he found a suitable place. His was a Ford Escape. It was a station wagon with tinted glass. He had to hide it under some cloth or rug. He needed to get rid of it soon. Leave it in the boot long enough, he was bound to be caught. He took his vehicle to work. They may question him there too. But at least he can give a rational explanation, unlike with Lakshmy.

He was driving past Ulsoor Lake. The thought crossed his mind: should he dump it in the lake? Even to do that he would have to come in the middle of the night. People will ask him what he was doing. If they suspected he was a terrorist he would lose his job. He rued having brought this upon himself. Why the hell did he bring out the first bit from the bushes? From then onwards the die had been cast. The curse of

Ravana was following him. He thought it was over but yesterday's phone call had put paid to that.

Radhika lived in Corporation colony. It was a modest rented house. The children were at school. Soon they were going to boarding school. She did shift duty in the ICU. She was off for the afternoon. She just wanted this metal burden to be out of her life. She was divorced. Her mother lived with her.

She was pretty. She was a bit on the dark side but had a body to die for. She had worked out regularly and maintained her fitness. She had been an athlete at school and university. She was tall for an Indian woman at five and a half feet. She had a beautiful face. She had cut her hair at shoulder length. She wore a green Chiffon Sari with matching sleeveless blouse. She looked very sexy even without any make up.

Sunil was in a quandary. He did not know what to take, if at all. Should he buy her flowers? That will give the wrong signal. What about chocolates? He was a fitness freak himself and did not want to give calories to anyone. Carbs are the new nicotine, he had read. Should he go empty handed? That would not be nice, since she had done him a favour. Finally, he settled on fruits. Bananas and oranges, he thought, could also be misconstrued! He said to himself why am I getting ahead of myself. I will just say thank you and take the stuff, put it in my boot, and get the hell out of there.

"Come on in," said Radhika. "Thank you for coming so promptly. I was worried what I would do with those things."

"I am the one who should thank you for carrying the stuff. And apologies for all the inconvenience."

"Actually it is not an inconvenience. I quite enjoyed seeing those idiots tear their hair out trying to figure out what they were. By the way, what are they? And why are you interested in them?"

Sunil explained to her about all that happened in Sri Lanka. He said, "Quite frankly I am over it. At that time, Ravana seemed very real. Now I think it was all just our imagination. We indulged in some fantasy. It's over now. All I need to do is to safely dispose of them."

"It is funny you tell about the dreams." said Radhika, placing a cup of tea in front of him. "Ever since I have had them I am having dreams of these monsters you describe. I think there is something to it. You should investigate."

Saying this she looked at him with pleading eyes. She was still standing. She looked very attractive. She did not want all her labour to go waste. She was curious as to what this all meant. She needed to know.

"I will do my best," said Sunil, getting up. He was shown where the two metal fragments were and he promptly collected them and placed them on the floor of his car boot. Radhika gave him some jute bags to cover them over. They were quite flat and with the tinted glass, they were not so visible from outside. I may get away with this one thought Sunil.

Radhika interrupted his thought process. "Does Lakshmy know you have come here?"

"No" said Sunil. Their eyes exchanged glances. They both knew something changed in their relationship at that instant.

Radhika had an expression of victory in her eyes. She knew she had one up on her friend Lakshmy. It was not that she had designs on Sunil. She had always been the flirtatious one while Lakshmy was the quiet one. Though they had been good friends, they did have an undercurrent of slight competition. When Radhika's marriage failed, she had felt that the whole world was thinking that she was a loser. She avoided contact with most of her family and friends including Lakshmy. Now Lakshmy's husband had visited her without his wife's knowledge. So much for successful marriages, she thought. When the husband and wife have secrets from each other how honest is their relationship? When she saw these subtle issues between other couples, it made her feel better. At least she was honest to herself.

Sunil's eyes had an expression of guilt. That of a thief caught in the act. The veneer of respectful distance between them was gone in a blink of an eye. Both knew it. He knew that their relationship was never going to be the same again.

He was glad to be home. He was exhausted. The effects of doing something on the sly can be draining. He knew that he was just one minute away from disaster as long as the 'contraband' remained in his possession. However, he did not know how to get out of the situation.

The next day passed as usual. Sunil was on an edge all day. He could not concentrate on his job. He had to find a solution for the issue soon before it blew up on him. The previous night he was tossing and turning in his bed for a long time, deep in thought. Lakshmy's advances went unnoticed, causing her to wonder what was going on with her husband. He was behaving strangely. She suspected something was up. She in fact asked him what was going on. She was not convinced with his denial that everything was fine. Then the demons had returned in his dream. Now he understood. The demons would keep bothering the person in possession of the artefacts until they did something about it.

Deep in thought, he drove to pick up Ajay from school to take him to tennis. The tennis racquets were usually placed in the boot. This time he put them in the back seat. When he was driving, he was suddenly brought back to the real world by Ajay's voice. "Dad what is that noise in the back of the car?" Yes, there was a noise of metal clanging.

"I need to get it checked by the mechanic tomorrow," said Sunil. The car is giving trouble lately.

Saved by the bell! Literally! Yes just then there was the alarm ringing out at the railway crossing.

"These trains always come in the way!" Sunil was happy to change the topic, thankful to Indian railways for the timely intervention.

He escaped that time. He needed to act fast. Should he fess up to Lakshmy, come clean and finish this agony? Or should he continue to hide things, hoping that he would never be caught. A logical brain would have selected the former option. They say 'aapad kaale vipareeta buddhi.' When the time comes even the best of brains, make simple mistakes.

So he decided to conceal this from Lakshmy. May be he would tell her after a year or two, when the emotion has been taken away from the situation. If he told now it would only lead to a flare up, he reckoned.

The next day he received a call in the evening, just before knocking off for the day. It was from Radhika. Now she had his mobile number. He was uncomfortable receiving calls from this woman. It was not that he did not like to talk to her. He was afraid of being caught by his wife. A few days had passed and his dreams had continued. Hers had stopped.

"What have you done with it?" Radhika told him that the dreams had stopped the moment the artefacts left her home. He told her his dreams had resumed.

"This is weird. We need to find out more about it," she said. "Can you get them analysed by a metallurgist?"

Why didn't he think of it? The metal was very hard but very light at the same time. Is that some new metal or alloy? Who can analyse and find out? He could not think of anyone off the top of his head but he knew this was the right approach. Once he found out what it was, he can either discard it as junk or if it turned out to be something useful, he can take credit for it. May be a Bharat Rathna or even the Nobel Prize! He chided himself for being so naive. However, he knew what he should do.

He asked his friends at the air force about who would analyse metals, without actually telling why. One of his colleagues, Rashid, laughed at him. He slapped his back and said, "I can't believe you didn't think of NAL! It is not far from where we are!"

An electric wave went off in Sunil's brain. Yes the National Aerospace Laboratories! They were in Airport Rd, Kodihalli. It was not far from the Defence Colony. Why didn't he think of it earlier? That will solve the immediate problem of finding a place for Ravana's junk. It may throw up some answers that may interest history buffs. If they were lucky, they may stumble upon some scientific discovery.

The Indian government machinery is such that if one department wants to coordinate with another, they had to go through the higher authorities, and that would mean more paper work, more red tape and a lot of delays. How could he circumvent all this? He was a government employee. There was a chain of command. Any breach in protocol could land him in serious trouble.

That evening when Radhika called, he told her about this. Her calls were becoming more frequent. Though he did not encourage her in the beginning, he was actually beginning to enjoy talking to her. He began to look forward to the calls. She was witty. At first, the calls were only about Ravana and the metal. Then they started talking about other things too. He knew he was being sucked into a vacuum. He did not want to go there. He did not want to stop either. It was like a firefly being drawn to a flame. When forces of nature are at work, who can stop them?

"May be I know someone at NAL! One of my friends' husbands is a scientist in an aerospace agency of some sort."

The next day she came back with the news that this person was indeed at the NAL. This meant he had to take the contraption back to Radhika. He felt like a thief covering his tracks. He needed to have an excuse for the work place. Then he needed to make sure he was not caught on CCTV. He should not be stopped by traffic police. He was not doing anything illegal but still he was apprehensive of any evidence left behind that could come back to haunt him. We are living in times of Orwell's Nineteen Eighty Four. Our cities are fortresses with electronic eyes everywhere. No one can do anything without the fear of being noticed.

He visited Radhika that afternoon. This was becoming too frequent. He would get rid of the stuff and end this whole thing. So he thought. Not so easily. Radhika did not want to take this to NAL herself. Instead, she wanted Sunil to go with her on an appointed day. He was still stuck with the dreams and the odd metal. He did not mind, as this would prolong the contact with this woman.

The next day at 10 o'clock, they had arranged to meet Mr Rangarajan, a scientist at NAL. The wife of Dr Rangarajan worked with Radhika. He happened to be a metallurgist. He was a PhD doctor. This was the type of scientist they were looking for.

The security at NAL was stringent. They required photo ID and took photographs of all visitors at the reception. Then the employee would come out to meet them. This meant they could not take their cargo in for his inspection. All the while Sunil was worried about building up incriminating evidence connecting him to Radhika. Having got into the water he had to swim somehow.

They parked at the corner of the street. There was a large tree and some street vendors. They decided it was ok to leave the car there. It was around midmorning and some of the shops were just opening. After a half hour wait Rangarajan came to the reception. He was a grey haired bespectacled man. He had spent a career in government service as a scientist. They went into an adjacent building. Visitors were not allowed inside the main compound for security reasons.

Dr Rangarajan listened intently. He was sceptical. Many people have claimed to have made new discoveries. Most of them turned out to be phonies or false alarmists. Nevertheless, he did not want to dismiss Sunil, as he was a Kargil veteran. To be polite he agreed to do his best. He doubted if anything would come of it.

"Where is the material?" asked Rangarajan. They said it was in his car. That would add another complexity. Vehicles were not allowed into the compound unless they belonged to NAL.

"How bulky is it?" asked the scientist.

"It is big but it is light," said Sunil. Dr Rangarajan was not the athletic type. He was thin and frail. How is he going to carry these two bulky metal objects? They will not allow Sunil to go in.

"Let me show them to you." All three of them walked back towards the Ford Escape. While they were gone, there had been bird droppings on the windshield. Sunil ignored that and opened the boot.

"I don't think I can carry them," said the scientist. They looked very heavy.

"Believe me. They are light." Saying this Sunil effortlessly lifted both pieces together.

"You want to try?" he asked, urging Dr Rangarajan to take one of them. The reluctant man took one of the pieces from Sunil.

"This is unbelievable! What is the material?" asked Rangarajan. He did not expect this to be so light. Now he doubted if this was just some hollow object with metallic exterior. But it did feel solid.

The next problem was that all objects taken into NAL would need to be X rayed and cleared by security. Dr Rangarajan was a stickler for procedure. A lifetime in government service will make anyone pedantic. He just wanted all paperwork to be properly documented. He asked Sunil to get a letter from the air force academy requesting the analysis of this material.

They left. Just as they had walked to the top of the road, an excited Rangarajan came running behind them. They thought that they had done something wrong, or that he had found another rule and another form to be filled.

He was excited and breathless from running. He said between short breaths "What have you given us? Are you sure it is an ancient relic and not something from science fiction?"

"Why do you ask?" said Radhika.

"For a start those two metal pieces are not showing up on X rays!" said the Scientist.

"What does that mean?" asked Radhika.

"They are invisible to X rays. They shouldn't be. But they are. People have been working on ways to absorb, bend or refract rays that would make the material invisible. No one has found the perfect way yet. What you have brought is completely invisible to X rays."

"Oh! That means it was from a technologically advanced civilization?" asked Sunil.

"I don't know yet. I think we are only at the beginning of unravelling the properties of these items. It is very interesting. Thank you very much for bringing it to us." Dr Rangarajan was thrilled.

With that, he promised to have some results soon.

12

Having got rid of Ravana's apparatus they felt a sense of great relief. They also had a feeling of anticipation. In life there come periods of time when you feel you are on the cusp of something big. There is eager waiting. Often times the expected outcome doesn't materialise or is less enjoyable than originally thought. That doesn't prevent the human mind from going on imaginary fantasies. In many ways, this period of waiting is more enjoyable than the ultimate result. This is a period when the human mind is at its creative best. It is very fertile and innovative. It is also open to romance during these periods.

Free of the monster dreams, free of the burden of carrying the 'contraband' in the car boot, free of the worry of the possibility of getting caught, and expecting the NAL to come up with something great, Sunil was at his passionate best. Lakshmy was surprised at his fervour. "What is going on?" she asked. "You seemed disinterested and distracted for some time and now you seem to be just the opposite."

Not that she complained about the extra attention she was receiving. However, as any married female will testify, any change in the husband's behaviour could mean something is going on in his life. The worst fear of any woman is an affair. Lakshmy wondered if the changes in Sunil meant the very thing that she dreaded was happening right now. She was on high alert. She paid more attention to his movements and his communications, without appearing to be spying.

Sunil was more relaxed than before. He did not really have a reason to meet or talk to Radhika now. Technically, that is. Call it middle age crisis or boredom with routine. He was interested in continuing this relationship. It is only platonic, he told himself. However, Radhika's calls gave him something to look forward to. How platonic is a relationship when one shares something with another person that he doesn't wish to tell his partner?

Initially the conversations revolved around the Ravana artefacts and the dreams. Now that Dr Rangarajan had expressed astonishment at the properties of the material, they discussed possibilities as to what it could be. Could it be possible that this was from a much later period and had nothing to do with Ravana? The talks invariably went to other topics. They shared their successes and frustrations in their daily lives. Sunil just needed someone to listen to the sometimes exaggerated descriptions of his exploits without the put-downs. Radhika was fulfilling this unmet need in Sunil's life. It is very easy to listen to someone when you are not living under the same roof as that person. There are no shared chores and no responsibilities. It is easy to put on your best mask when you meet the person. This can't be done twenty four hours of the day.

However, they were getting closer. Still nothing physical happened. On the contrary, Sunil seemed to be more charged in his relationship with Lakshmy. Perhaps the so-called platonic friendships help people to recharge their batteries before going back to their permanent partners.

It was a month before Rangarajan called. Even then, he had minimal news only. The specimen items were interesting. They had been sent to another lab for further analysis. He still wanted Sunil's department to complete the paper work. Every i should be dotted.

He did ask if there was any more material. Only then did Sunil remember the wheel. Radhika had not seen the wheel and it had been lying idle in Sunil's garage ever since they returned from Sri Lanka.

He mentioned the wheel to Lakshmy. "What about it?" she asked. "Aren't you happy to just forget about the whole thing and move on? Didn't you see how our holiday was spoilt by this sort of nonsense?"

It was now or never for Sunil. He had a chance to confess to Lakshmy that he had been in contact with Radhika and that the specimens were sent for further analysis. In any case, he had not crossed any line. He had not gone beyond a point of no return. All he had to do was to bring Lakshmy into his confidence and team up with her.

The other option was to keep pursuing this project behind Lakshmy's back and deal with the consequences if and when she found out. This way he was postponing an immediate confrontation but was risking a more serious conflagration at a later date. He had not done anything illegal or immoral up to that point.

Sunil's priority was to avoid confrontation and keep the peace. So he said "Ok let me dispose of that tyre. It is just occupying space in the garage."

It really wasn't taking up space but Lakshmy was glad to get rid of it and put all their holiday horrors behind them. "Now that you reminded me I can take it to a tyre warehouse where they trade in second hand tyres," she offered.

"It is not exactly a tyre in the normal sense. It is a wheel made of plastic or similar material. Let me take it to the air force dump."

That settled the issue for the time being. Sunil had his way, and his wheel. Lakshmy was happy to be clear of the last remnant of their weird experience. With the passage of time, they could completely forget about this episode. Forget Ravana forever. Forget about the mystical under world of Sri Lankan culture. She wanted to lead a normal life.

He took the wheel and placed it in the back seat. Now he had another reason to meet Radhika. When they met Dr Rangarajan this time, he was careful not to park under the tree where the birds were. The good doctor came to their car to inspect this new specimen. He told them the metal objects had been sent for further testing as it involved complicated analysis. He was happy to look at other evidence presumably related to the same source. When he looked at the wheel, he said immediately "This is made of a polymer. It needs to be analysed in a spectrum laboratory. I suggest you send it to Delhi for this."

It was beyond the capabilities of his laboratory and he did not want to take on any work that was outside the scope of his department and especially when it was not official work. By the way, he had not received the inter-departmental request regarding the earlier samples and he was anxious that his job might be on line if proper protocol was not followed.

He did acknowledge that the earlier samples had produced some remarkable results and the discovery could be ground breaking.

They were both disappointed that Dr Rangarajan did not receive the wheel for analysis. They went into a nearby cafe for some chai tea and to ruminate on the events, and perhaps plan the next step. This was the first time they were out in a public place together. Sunil's heart was racing. Guilt conscience, he told himself. You haven't done anything wrong. So why do you feel bad, he told himself.

"I have a friend from USA. He is visiting us shortly. Let us see if he can take it back with him for testing over there." Radhika had doctor friends all over the world. There were many acquaintances during the course of her training abroad. She had kept in touch.

He looked intently at Radhika. Then he said slowly "Radhika I don't know what we will find but there is a possibility that these apparatuses can have military applications. They may or may not be from Ravana. But if they do have military uses I don't want anyone else to know about these." Being a military man, he was always conscious of security. It was not personal security alone. It was security of information too. Knowledge is power they say. What started as a simple distraction may turn out to be of great importance for national security.

"Ok ok I will not involve others in this. It is our little secret heh!" Radhika winked at him. "Does Lakshmy know about this?"

"No" said Sunil abruptly, averting her glance. He knew she had him on this one.

"Oh Mr Mishra! So you mean to say your dear wife Lakshmy does not know this secret which may be of national importance but I, Radhika, a third party knows about it?" She wanted to drive home this fact. This would define their future relationship. She enjoyed his discomfiture very much.

"I will tell her when it is opportune." Sunil was looking beyond her, not daring to look at her in the eye.

"Ok in that case, because you are not telling your wife, I will not tell my boyfriends." She was teasing him.

"Do you have a boyfriend?" There was a pang of jealousy in his voice.

"Why can't I have boyfriends? I am single now. Even you are a boyfriend!" Radhika was having fun at his expense. Was she just teasing or was she testing the waters? Oh the games they play!

Poor Sunil was worried that he was developing feelings for this gorgeous woman. Who would not? She was pretty, athletic and witty. Above all, she seemed to have attitude and class. It was not that Lakshmy lacked in anything. But she was always preoccupied with family affairs. She was not the sort for adventure. Who knows how Radhika was to her ex-husband. Perhaps she was like Lakshmy. Now she is unfettered and is able to do things, that she was not doing with her husband. That may be why her relationship broke down. Otherwise why would anyone not want to be with this woman in front of him?

Sunil chided himself for allowing his mind to wander. He was not looking for an affair. He certainly liked her company and the circumstances that had brought her into this project. He wanted to see it through to the finish. That was all. He shouldn't get ahead of himself. Once he got to the bottom of this Ravana business, he would explain everything to Lakshmy.

Both of them were conscious of prying eyes. Bangalore may have grown into a sprawling city; people may be westernised; but they still would notice and talk about a man and a woman who were not husband and wife, meeting like lovers. Who could predict who may walk in on them? So they decided to call it for the day. Sunil was going to try his friends in Delhi to see if they could find anyone to analyse this. He had to be careful not to divulge too much information. He tried his air force contacts first. Without giving too much detail, he just told them he wanted a polymer to be analysed to find out what material it was.

He had to enlist the support of his senior, Air Commodore Mohan Gupta. Mr Gupta was only too happy to help. He left the wheel in the office. He told Lakshmy that he had disposed of it. Before long, it was dispatched by secure mail to Delhi.

Radhika and Sunil continued to communicate. She would call every afternoon. His colleagues were beginning to wonder whether he was up to something fishy. However, like true military men they were used to unquestioning loyalty to their comrades. For his part, he made sure all his call history was deleted each evening. He had told Radhika not to text him. Well in this electronic age, how can you erase your tracks? Everything you do is etched permanently in cyberspace. Some cults teach you that God knows all your thoughts and all these are recorded permanently. Thought crime is as bad as actual crime, they teach. Whether thoughts are recorded or not the actions are recorded and have the habit of surfacing in the most unexpected places at the most inopportune times. Anyone following WikiLeaks and US elections would testify to this.

13

Another month passed by. The phone calls continued. But they did not meet. Radhika hinted that she might have a boyfriend. Sunil did not like the idea. He steered the conversation away from the topic each time it popped up. It was entirely possible that she was just teasing him. Why was he feeling possessive? Who is he to her to feel possessive? What can he offer her by way of stability or security? Nothing! Then how can he feel jealous if she had other men. He could not understand himself. May be it was the cave man instinct. The instinct that makes a lion mark its territory. Only here the territory did not belong to him.

Then the call came, this time from Dr Rangarajan himself. Usually he communicated through Radhika. For some reason he had deemed it fit to call Sunil directly. This must be important. He invited Sunil and his superior Gupta for a conference. Sunil asked if he could bring Radhika along. This request was politely refused.

They were asked to come to NAL on the appointed day, at 8 am. It was a Tuesday. Sunil was asked to set aside the whole day. No one was to be told about this meeting. It was shrouded in secrecy. Sunil was told this meeting was connected to national security.

At NAL, they were screened as usual but this time they were invited into the compound, into a separate building. There was a high level of security. Only those cleared by the high command were allowed in.

There was a large conference room. All the attendees were sworn to secrecy. This was a highly sensitive meeting, they were told. The air force commander was to attend in the afternoon. Most of the men were in uniforms. The ones in civilian clothes were probably scientists, Sunil guessed.

The director of NAL presided. There were about 15 people in all. "Friends," said the director. "This is an important day in the history of the NAL. Indeed, it is an important day for Bharat! We are indebted to group captain Sunil Mishra for bringing us two objects that he found in Sri Lanka. His story, if we can believe it, points to these fragments being part of Ravana's Pushpaka Vimana. I am a Muslim and I have not believed in the authenticity of Ramayana until now. But if it is indeed from Ravana's aircraft, he must've been a very good scientist!"

With this preamble, he invited Sunil to tell the audience briefly what he found and how he chanced upon it. Then it was Dr Rangarajan's turn at the podium. In his soft spoken, self-effacing way, the good doctor started to explain their findings.

"When Mr Mishra brought these samples I did not think they were of any importance." He paused and smiled at Sunil. "I only agreed to test these as his lady friend is known to my wife."

Sunil looked downwards. He could not face Gupta's questioning eyes. Mm that explains the phone calls, thought Gupta.

"In any case the first indication that we were onto something was when we tried to x ray these for security clearance. We were astounded when these objects were invisible to x ray. We couldn't believe it. Then we systematically tested the structure and the nature of the specimens. We were very surprised by what we found." He paused to take a sip if water. Everyone was hanging by every word coming out of his mouth. He was not in any hurry to spill the beans. "I have to explain in basic terms and cut out the technical jargon. But if any of you cannot follow, please feel free to interrupt me."

"Firstly the material was not a simple metal object as we originally thought. Nor was it an alloy." He paused for effect. If he was hoping to get all their attention he succeeded hundred and fifty percent. Everyone was holding his or her breath.

"This was a composite material of a type that we have only seen in this millennium, that is, well after year 2000. These are called metamaterials. Metamaterials are composite interwoven collection of material that manipulate the way electromagnetic waves interact with the material, and this can range from very high frequency gamma rays to the extremely low frequency waves. I will explain about frequency and wavelengths in a minute. The effect of this is to make the object invisible. People have been trying to make invisible cloaks for some time now. They have only succeeded in making some crude contraptions.

"But the material sample provided to us shows a highly refined technology which we didn't know exists. The two objects that you brought were not actually the wings of a plane or the rotor blades of a motor. We think they are part of an apparatus that is designed to hide objects from radars, x ray machines and indeed the visual spectrum.

"Not only that. We also found a metal that was used in the manufacture of this metamaterial that has not yet been discovered in science. Because of this discovery, we are going to have to rewrite the periodic table.

"This finding is shocking. It is going to turn science on its head. If it was indeed from Ravana's time then we have to admit that science was far more advanced then, than it is now.

"I will explain the details shortly. Another finding that is going to rewrite history is that there was some DNA material on these samples. We are analysing that but preliminary results point to a species that may be slightly different to Homo sapiens. With some luck, we may be able to clone Ravana's people. That is not our primary objective, however.

"Basically we are having this meeting because our findings will have profound implications for military technology. We can make superior aircraft using this advanced methodology. And we have to prevent this knowledge from falling in the hands of the enemy."

He then went on to explain about electromagnetic waves. Dr Rangarajan was very patient. He said, "Light consists of particles and waves. Perhaps it was this duality that the Chinese called Yin and Yang, and the Hindus called Shiva and Shakti. The wave consists of electric and magnetic fields. These electromagnetic waves can be of any wavelength. When it is visible to the eye, we call it the visual spectrum. But the wave lengths can be below or above the visual spectrum in which case the human eye cannot see them."

"At this stage let me explain the frequency and wavelength. The greater the energy of a wave, the greater the frequency of the oscillation. It follows that greater the energy, the shorter the wavelength because frequency and wavelength are inversely related. When one goes up the other goes down.

"When you consider the visual spectrum, which we know as VIBGYOR, violet has the shortest wave length and therefore the highest frequency which means more energy. Ultraviolet spectrum consists of even more energy. Beyond this are the x rays and gamma rays. At the other end of the spectrum, the infrared rays have longer wavelengths and lower frequency. Then we have microwaves and radio waves.

"Every object emits electromagnetic waves. It also modifies the waves that reach it from other sources. This is by reflection, refraction, absorption and so on.

"Just like human eyes can see a light that comes from the objects, we can detect waves in the spectrum on either side using special techniques. So all objects should be visible in some form of imagery. For this, we need emitted or reflected beams from the object. Imagine if the waves are made to pass around the object and not distorted in any way? Then we won't see the object. That is what the metamaterials aim to do. If we succeed in that, planes can be flown into enemy territory without being detected by radar or satellites. Nor will they be visible to the naked eye.

"The specimens you brought back from Sri Lanka were not parts of a motor or wings or propellers. They are part of a system of fans fitted around the aircraft. When they are operated at a certain frequency, they create a field with zero refractive index around the aircraft. The electromagnetic waves will just flow around the aircraft without being altered. It would be like water flowing around a pebble in a stream.

"If we succeed in replicating Ravana's idea we can make planes that will fly deep into enemy territory without being detected. They won't be seen even if they are directly over your head.

"This is a dream machine for any military. We have been authorized to go full steam ahead in developing this further. It may take a couple of years but we are confident we will succeed in this endeavour."

It was a lot to take in. The government had given its full backing. In fact, there was bipartisan consensus, with the opposition leader being taken into confidence. Sunil couldn't believe it. What had started as a trivial pursuit had led to some major development. No wonder Ravana was persistent in his efforts. He wanted the world to know about his glorious machine. Especially he wanted Bharat to know. He felt that they were the rightful heirs to Sita, the queen of his heart. He wanted to help them.

They had tea before the next session. Everyone seemed spellbound by the revelations. All the military high command lined up to congratulate Sunil and Rangarajan. It was a discovery that could potentially make India a military super power. It was not that they were craving for world dominance. They could at least be one-step ahead of their belligerent neighbours Pakistan and China with whom they had fought wars in the past.

They convened the next session after a bit of banter. Again, Rangarajan took the stage. People were wondering what else he was going to say. It was already a day filled with wonders. What more can he add. What he told them took them from astonishment to stupendous amazement. They could only wonder in awe of the technology of the ancients. Were they from outer space? Was there a far more advanced civilization that has become extinct? They were left with a million questions.

He began, in his usual fashion, from the basics. He said, "When we characterize metals we look at several patterns. Their density or specific gravity, tensile strength, thermal expansion properties, corrosion resistance, conductivity, reflectivity, magnetizing properties, malleability, joinability, and last but not the least, potential toxicity to humans. When we build aircraft, we need to use material that is light but sturdy with optimum properties in all the categories mentioned. The aircraft were built using Aluminium. Now there are composite materials that are better than Aluminium that can be used for aircraft building."

"The samples you gave us were not made of just one material. As I mentioned before, they were metamaterial using many metal and non-metal components. So we went about analysing each constituent element. What we found was amazing.

While all the other elements were ordinary substances that we use already, there was one that was different. In fact, we have never seen that before. It has not been described before. In short, it is a new element! We have analysed it and we have comprehensively proven that it is new element that has never been found before. We have named it Ravanium in honour of Mr Ravana. With the discovery of Ravanium we have to change a lot of things in our understanding of the elements and indeed of atoms. There is going to be a paradigm shift. The periodic table as it is known today will be shredded. But we don't want to publicise our discovery. Publicity will bring fame and perhaps even the Nobel Prize. However, it will not serve our national interests. So we have decided to keep it a secret. This metal has wonderful properties. First let me explain to you about atoms and atomic weight.

"The nucleus of the atom comprises of protons and neutrons. Protons are the positive charge. The number of protons determines the atomic number. The neutrons do not have a charge and the number of neutrons tends to be roughly equal to the number of protons. This is not always the case. Therefore, when there are more neutrons to the same number of protons they are called isotopes. There cannot be more protons than neutrons as the charged particles will repel each other and become unstable without equal or more number of the neutral neutrons."

"Mendeleev organised the 63 then known elements into a periodic table, meaning there was recurring pattern of behaviour periodically according to atomic weight. Later it was realised that the behaviour depended on the atomic number and not the atomic weight. The atomic weight depended on the number of neutrons and protons together. The atomic number depends on the number of protons only.

"What started as a table with 63 elements now has 118 elements. So man is discovering more elements all the time. Usually the atomic number goes up with each discovery.

"The new substance that we isolated had a lot of properties of Aluminium. Then we analysed it to see if it is a known material. It wasn't. The results surprised us. Aluminium has an atomic number of 13 and an atomic weight of 26.961. We got an atomic weight of 13.48, which does not correspond to any known element. On further analysis, we found that there are subatomic particles other than protons and neutrons in the Universe. Ravanium is made up of 13 protonids and 13 neutronids.

"We know of the Large Hadron Collider and Higgs boson etc. People have been looking for these subatomic particles in extensive expensive experiments. But in Ravanium, we think we have found these in nature without the need to artificially create them. Ravana must have had his metal in abundance. He has used quite a lot of this in those two specimens you gave us. We think he would have built his aircraft using the same metal because its properties are ideal. We need to look for the deposits of Ravanium. We think by using satellite spectroscopy we can sweep large areas to look for any sign of this metal. If the deposits are close enough to the surface, we should be able to locate these.

"One of the suggestions is that these deposits have not been found because they are buried under the snow. Antarctica is the obvious place to look for them. The other possibility is the Himalayas. The Himalayas rose to these spectacular heights due to large tectonic shifts according to traditional wisdom. It is possible that there may have been nuclear events that created so much energy as to cause this huge mountain range to rise up. Where there are nuclear events there are bound to be subatomic particles thrown around. These may have given rise to Ravanium and even more elements like that.

"We know that Mr Ravana got into trouble with Lord Shiva trying to dig up Mount Kailash. We don't know why he did that. It is said that he came in his Pushpaka Vimana and then tried to dig up at the base of the mountain. It is entirely possible that he came to explore for this metal, which we have called Ravanium.

"If our findings are confirmed it will change the entire science of chemistry. The periodic table will need to be altered radically.

"Gentlemen," he said. We are living in an exciting era. We are thrilled with these findings. Yet we need to be cautious. It is very tempting to report this to the international scientific fraternity. We need to think. If the findings are going to give us a military advantage, we should hold onto this information. If we use this properly we can have a twenty year military advantage over all other countries, including the United States."

It left them dazed. Especially Sunil could not believe this was happening in reality. It was like a science fiction movie. Something like Star Wars. If this was true, then the Puranas could also be true. Brahmastra and all the other weapons of mass destruction could have been atomic weapons. Perhaps that was what caused that highly evolved civilization to perish. The possibilities were endless. Inter galactic travel may have actually taken place.

"One final note. We did recover some DNA from these samples. These could have been contaminants. We did not pay too much attention to that. However, we sent it for testing for completion. As a government agency, we could not leave anything unattended. If it were just human or animal DNA, it would not have been big news. But what we found shocked us. There were humanoid features of course but there were important differences. We think that belongs to another human like species. I am not an expert on DNA but my colleagues tell me that they may be able to clone that. I am not sure how successful they will be but even if they cannot clone that species, we think the Pushpaka Vimana had contact with another species. It may be that Ravana belonged to that species. Or it may be that he had servants and warriors from another species, just like our own Rama had Sugreeva's army helping him."

That was the icing on the cake. Besides the real possibility of helping India become the foremost super power in the world, the fact that the events described in Ramayana may have actually happened left everyone dizzy.

14

From that day onwards Sunil's problems multiplied. Now he had to hide these new revelations from Radhika. And he had to hide everything from Lakshmy. If that was not enough, every time he received a phone call Mr Gupta would give him a sarcastic knowing smile, as if to say it is ok, we all do it too! He only hoped that this should end soon so that he could live his normal life again.

Sunil did not tell Radhika anything about the meeting but the topic came up again when she asked him whether she should call Dr Rangarajan. She was curious to find out if they came up with any answers. He quickly changed the topic saying these scientists take their own time and did not like to be pestered. He was able to ward her off for another month or so. At that time, the results from the testing of the wheel came back. This came through official air force channels. Again, Sunil was summoned for a meeting. He was asked to come to Delhi along with his superiors.

He was accommodated in the air force mess, and taken to Vayu Bhawan, in Motilal Nehru Marg. Again, it was a meeting around a long rectangular table. Sunil was being treated as a hero. Well, hero of sorts. Because he could not take his family with him to see him being praised and cherished. Nor could he even tell Lakshmy why he was going to the capital. He just made up some excuse and told her it was an official meeting. She was worried that he was going to be sent to the front line again.

Sunil was surprised to see that the Commander of the air force was himself present. They must be taking this very seriously, he thought. Then the commander said after the initial introductions and salutations, "So group captain Sunil Mishra, you are saying you found this wheel while on holiday in Sri Lanka. Can you tell us more about the circumstances that led to this finding please?"

Sunil was nervous. Even when he was honoured for his bravery in Kargil he did not feel this level of anxiety. Surely, they would not have called me to Delhi if there was nothing in this. In addition, the air force chief wouldn't have attended in person if this was trivial.

He started with the story of the metal artefacts, the dreams, the demons and so on. Then he described how his wife Lakshmy was swept away in a waterfall in Hasalaka, which was close to what was supposed to be Ravana's airport. He described how she went missing for hours and how she was found upstream from the falls, completely unhurt, floating on this wheel. Everyone listened to his story intently. Some had unbelieving but polite facial expressions. The incredible story could not be taken at face value. Who believes that Ramayana really happened? Even if it did, it was a skirmish between two Stone Age gangs; one even had monkeys among them. At the most, they would have had spears and arrows. Aircraft? You must be joking!

Then the scientist made a presentation. He introduced himself as Professor Chandrasekhar Rao from CSIR, Council of Scientific and Industrial Research. He specialised in structure of polymers. He said "Gentlemen, what I am going to tell you is going to surprise you. We analysed the wheel for its composition. We found it to be made of a polymer that we have not seen before. As you know polymers are organic structures made of repetitive occurrence of the same molecule, connected by covalent bonds. In lay terms what we call plastic in general are all polymers. We have Nylon, Polyester, and Polyurethane and so on. This particular material that the wheel is made of, is a polymer with interconnected lattice of molecules, so much so that it is like a net, if you can imagine a three dimensional net. It is porous but these pores are microscopic. The pores are so small that even water molecule cannot pass through them. Oxygen and Nitrogen, not to mention Hydrogen can pass through the pores. As you know, our atmosphere is made up of nearly 80% Nitrogen. The effect of the pores is that through capillary action there is a constant flow of air through the material, which is impermeable to water. The structure of the molecule is such that this flow of air will be in one direction only. In effect, this will keep a steady stream of air flowing through this wheel, which in turn will minimise friction between the wheel and the surface on which it is moving. Once the initial momentum has been gained, this elimination of friction will enable the vehicle to reach very high speed on land. There will be minimal loss of energy as heat. The whole machine will be fuel-efficient and be able to propel itself to extremely high velocities.

"I do not want to bore you with the chemical structure etc. but this material is unique to science and we have decided to name it Ravanalon. It is porous, light and very hardy. I am not sure if this is from Ravana's era. It looks like we have brought some material from the twenty fifth century. It is so futuristic!"

The air force commander spoke next. "In industry, usually we would have applied for patent in the first instance, because this molecule is unique. We are debating whether we should actually do so or not. This polymer, if we can replicate it, will revolutionise our military vehicles, both land vehicles as well as aircraft. We do not want the enemy to know about the existence of this. Therefore, we are keeping this a secret. All of you are sworn to secrecy and as true patriots I expect you to maintain confidentiality at all times."

He then looked at Sunil. "Group captain Mishra, do you recall any other events during your holiday that may help us find more clues to this great machine that Ravana had?"

"Mm..ahh..I am trying to think Sir. Yes, there was another revelation. This time about the engine. The whole engine or parts of it may be hidden in a secret place. I was told where to learn about this place but I had completely forgotten to do this. Firstly, I did not believe in the Ravana story until the scientists confirmed that we are indeed on to something great. I did not want to go on a wild goose chase without a good reason. Now that we have confirmed the authenticity of at least part of the story, I will explore this lead if you give me permission."

"Please go ahead. We shall make everything available to you. All the resources of the government will be made available to you. However, remember this is a secret mission. You can't go with all guns blazing. Discretion is the key. So what is it that you want to follow? Do you need to go to Sri Lanka again?"

If you are a group captain and the air force commander even looks at you, you would have attained moksha or nirvana, depending on your religion. But here he was not only looking at him, he was also talking to him and pledging to make available all the necessary resources. Sunil was on cloud nine, almost literally. This must be heaven. Where is St. Peter?

Sunil bowed his head and said, "I am humbled by your offer, Sir! I need to go to Rameshwaram where the next clue is. If we are destined to uncover Ravana's secrets he will guide us, I am sure. After that we may need to go to Sri Lanka one more time."

"Do whatever that needs to be done. I will grant you official leave for as long as necessary. Because this is a discreet mission, I will not assign any detail to you. I will give you an encrypted communication set which will enable you to contact the Indian High Commissioner or the Military Attaché in Sri Lanka or contact me directly in an emergency. I will get our signals officer to train you how to use it."

With that, the meeting concluded. Sunil was asked to stay in Delhi for a couple of days more. He had a time trying to explain to Lakshmy what was going on without revealing sensitive information. She was upset that he was doing something without her knowledge. She thought he was having what every married woman dreads, an affair!

At the air force advanced communication command, they fitted a microchip to his cell phone. With a series of codes that he had to memorize, he could communicate directly with the three people mentioned by the air force commander. The phone lines used an encrypted bandwidth that could not be eves dropped on, or jammed, by foreign intelligence agencies. He was to use this mode of communication only when in desperate need. At other times, he should report to the nearest air force base using his usual identity card.

All his travel would be by usual public transport as special travel arrangements could lead to suspicion and scrutiny by spies.

He was back in Bangalore for a week before scheduling a trip to Rameshwaram. He tried his best to be normal to Lakshmy and the kids. The children were really missing their usually bubbly dad. He seemed to be preoccupied with something. Especially Ajay was missing Sunil's input. This was an age when father-son bonding will mould the future of the growing man. Every house chore was falling on Lakshmy. Even taking Ajay to tennis classes was thrust upon her.

The more evasive Sunil was with his answers, the more convinced that Lakshmy was that he was having an affair. Once a woman is convinced about this, it is hard to unconvince her. Every minute he was late, every unexplained phone call, every moment that he was lost in thought, in fact every action that Sunil did apart from sleep, became another of the solid evidence base that she was building up.

Sunil told her that he was called to the headquarters for special training. The training would last six weeks and he was going the following Monday.

That was it! All the tension that was building up in Lakshmy boiled over! She had a complete meltdown! This man is going on a honeymoon with this other woman! She screamed, cried, gnarled and beat his chest! How could he do this to her? How could he do this to the children? After a couple of days of this hysteria it took a visit from Mr Gupta and other colleagues to convince her that he was in fact going to Delhi for training. Of these, only Gupta knew where he was heading.

If dealing with Lakshmy was a major problem, fending off Radhika became another head ache. She knew that he was hiding something from her. She knew it was about the Ravana materials. She pointedly asked him, during the telephone calls what happened to the tests at NAL. Dr Rangarajan had deftly side stepped the issue by asking her to ask Sunil. That was very nice of the good doctor, thought Sunil. He is an artful dodger!

Finally, he agreed to meet Radhika. He owed her an explanation. After all, it was Radhika who carried the material to India, and it was she who introduced Dr Rangarajan. He thought he should tell her at least some sketchy details without giving out sensitive information. He owed it to her. So he agreed to meet her at a cafe in Ulsoor.

15

They met at a cafe. This was a boutique cafe. It was small. There were soft Ghazal songs being played in the background. It was lunchtime. They had agreed to have lunch together. They took the buffet option. With buffet, they could take more protein and fewer carbohydrates. Both were conscious of their diets, with the middle age flab threatening to raise its head in their middle regions. However much you try it is difficult to avoid the rich gravy of Indian curries. At least they could avoid eating a lot of rice.

After the initial exchange of the usual pleasantries, they served their meals and settled in a corner. They deliberately selected a restaurant that was a little out of the way. It was also small enough not to attract too many customers. Most customers appeared to be working people coming for a quick lunch. Some seemed to have come in small groups.

There was an inner recess where only couples seemed to sit. It was as though there was an unwritten law that this was a couple's area. In fact, there was a half curtain, which though it demarcated the area, did not provide much cover. There were a few couples. How many were just friends? How many were married to each other? How many were married to others, like Radhika and Sunil?

"Are you trying to avoid me?"

Radhika was waiting to tear into him. He was behaving weirdly of late. This is not the Sunil that had kept her enraptured with tales of Kargil and Ravana.

What has happened to the witty man of whom she had grown quite fond? Granted he was not her man. But they had become good friends. She expected friends to behave like friends. He can at least be warm and talkative like he normally is.

"Just busy with work Radhi" Sunil was on the defensive.

"Your phone was switched off for many days. I did not want to leave messages as that would risk Lakshmy finding out."

"I saw that you had called," said Sunil, meekly.

"Is it too much to expect an explanation?" Radhika was persistent. It is hard to get someone off your back if they are determined not to let you off, especially if that person is a woman.

"Ok I will tell you. It was an important meeting."

"Was it related to Ravana? Dr Rangarajan asked me to ask you!"

Just then, his cell phone rang. Excuse me, said Sunil, answering the call. He was thankful that he could get some respite from her interrogation. He had just come off a bout of vigorous questioning from Lakshmy. Now he had to face Radhika. For now, he would take this phone call, gladly!

He looked around to see if there was any area that was more private. However, there was nowhere to hide from Radhika. If he had walked out into the main area, there were many more people there. So he decided to talk in front of her. He wished he had lowered the volume earlier. It was too late now.

It was a call from the railway agent. He had booked to go from Bangalore to Madurai by train, and then take a rented vehicle to Rameshwaram. He had selected the Bengaluru Nagarcoil express, which left at 5.15pm. It would reach Madurai in the early hours of the morning. He wanted to spend a day in Madurai. He had always wanted to spend time in the city of temples. He thought he would treat himself for a day there. He could arrange a hire car from there, and leave for Rameshwaram early morning the next day. He wanted to finish his search in Rameshwaram and return as soon as he found what he was looking for. He had not booked his return journey. He wanted to leave that open until he accomplished his mission.

He wanted to book an AC two tier seat. They had added an AC two-tier compartment recently. All the seats had been taken. He was wait-listed for any sudden last minute cancellations. This was the travel agent calling him. There had been a booking for two people. The couple could not go due to some unforeseen circumstances. It was too late to cancel at the railways. They wanted someone to take both tickets.

"They will sell only if you buy both tickets Sir!" The agent insisted that he bought both or he would try someone else who would take them together.

"Ok I will take both tickets!" Sunil just did not want to go by non-AC compartment. The summer nights are quite hot. He realised that Radhika had been listening to him. There was no point in hiding about his trip.

"Does she know you are going?" She seemed to be asking all the tricky questions. He was like a rabbit caught in head lights. He had nowhere to hide.

"No," he muttered, in a barely audible whisper.

"So what is this all about?" Radhika was a hard customer. Sunil had already exhausted his reservoir of lies on Lakshmy. A man can only lie so much. After a certain point, his resistance crumbles and he gives up. He confesses.

"Ok ok I will tell you if you don't press for details. That Ravana thingy started as a joke but it looks like we have stumbled upon some great scientific discoveries. Please don't ask me until the investigations are complete."

He emphasised the word scientific, neglecting to tell that it was really military secrets that they had inadvertently uncovered.

"So what has that got to do with the trip to Rameshwaram?"

He could not hide from her. "I am not sure if I told you or not. In the final leg of our tour, we went to meet a hermit in Kathirgamam. He said the engine of the Pushpaka Vimana is hidden from the time of Ravana's slaying. Only a certain clan of priests in Rameshwaram know the information about the whereabouts. They memorise this information mechanically, as part of the rituals, without actually knowing the true significance!"

"Whoa! So those were parts of the Pushpaka Vimana? How nice of you to tell me, after making me carry that junk for you."

"By the way why are you going to Madurai by train? Why couldn't you have flown?"

Radhika's question was logical. In fact, Sunil himself was ruing the decision to go by train. The reason for this is that had he flown it was more likely that everyone including Lakshmy would have a record of his travel. With train journey, identity checks were less stringent. He wouldn't have had to explain all this to Radhika had he taken the straightforward but more public option.

While he was thinking what to say, the next question landed on him like a tonne of bricks. This was the killer blow. The selling point, one may say. Just three words. But how powerful words can be, when used in the opportune time. "Does she know?" These were the three fatal words. They sealed his fate.

"No," he said looking down, averting her eyes.

Who is she to him? Why should he allow her to aggressively quiz him like this? He didn't know why. He knew he was caught.

"I am coming with you!" Radhika said in a matter-of-factly manner. This was not a request. Rather it was a statement.

"What are you saying Radhika?" Sunil asked slowly. There was no conviction in his voice.

"You have two tickets. I just heard that. So, we are going together. Trust me you will be thankful to have an assistant like me. And don't worry I won't tell her." Her tone was decisive. There was not an iota of doubt. This was the verdict. And her will shall be done.

"What about your children?" Sunil still had some hope of getting out of this.

"They are with their father for the summer holidays. Don't worry about them."

In a way, Sunil liked having company. It will help to ward off the boredom during the travel. Then again, two brains will be better than one. Besides, she knew Tamil, as her mother was Tamil. That will come handy when they were searching in Rameshwaram. They were going to look for a needle in a haystack. Therefore, every bit of help was welcome.

That agreed, now Radhika took over. She booked two rooms under her name in a Madurai hotel. She was careful to avoid the five star hotels, instead settling for one of the clean but not so posh three star hotels near the Meenakshi Temple. She did not want to give any evidence that can be used to prove that they travelled together. Security at the smaller hotels was also quite strict but usually they did not keep computerised record of all the guests. She did not want Sunil to think that she had designs on him. Therefore, she booked two separate rooms.

On Sunil's part, it was abject surrender. He did not know the places in Tamil Nadu much. Radhika had the advantage of the language and local knowledge, having been to her maternal relatives' many times. Once he acceded to her request, or rather command, that she go with him, he left it to her to arrange the rest. The main condition was that they should not leave any incriminating evidence.

It was around 5 pm when they boarded the train. Sunil was dressed in a verti and shirt, and wore a red thilak on his forehead. He had to go to Radhika's place to change. Radhika wore traditional sari. They looked like a typical Tamil Brahmin couple. This entire disguise was to avert any prying eyes that may start a rumour.

Indian Railways is a gigantic organisation run by the central government. It is a wonder how it can run almost to the timetable, be kept fairly clean, and have a reasonably efficient booking system while upwards of 10000 trains carry 23 million passengers daily. In addition, it moves cargo of equally huge proportions. No wonder the Railways has its own Ranji Trophy cricket team. It must be equal to an Indian state. Sunil thought that Indian Railways were an icon of national pride when he saw how clean the trains were as they boarded.

The train started on time. The two-tier compartment contained partitioned areas that had bunk style cushioned benches. There were four in each area, arranged as the lower and upper berths. When the train started, there were four passengers for each such area, seated in pairs facing each other. As the evening progressed, and after dinner, two of the passengers would go to the upper berths while the other two used the lower berths. The whole area as well as the individual berths had curtains for privacy. Sunil was impressed by the ingenious design that was comfortable and efficient at the same time.

"Look here, they have plug points!" Radhika was excited as she connected her laptop. They even had free Wi-Fi on board. This was something that was not available in many Western countries. India built its economic resurgence on the computing power of its people. It was no wonder to see India take the lead in providing access to internet everywhere and at all times.

Radhika spent a lot of time on her face book. She controlled the urge to tell where she was or what she was doing. It was fashionable for her friends to post even their flight times and flight paths for the entire world to see. This time she had to hide her movements.

Sunil was worried that they would miss Madurai station. Radhika had brought home cooked food. They had some chai tea and said their good nights. Sunil took the upper berth. He set the alarm on his cell phone. He asked the railway attendant to alert them when the train approached Madurai. Yet he could not sleep. The arrival time was about 2.30 am. He dreaded missing his station and ending up in Nagarcoil in the morning. Radhika was not bothered about this possibility.

"Well if that happens we will just get a hire car and go directly to Rameshwaram," she said. It was usually the woman that worries about these finer details, but Radhika seemed nonchalant.

Sunil did not know when he dozed off but he woke up when his alarm went off at the same time as the railway attendant tapped his shoulder. Hmm the system works, he said to himself.

Two thirty am in Madurai. The city should have been deserted. Not so around the railway station area. Auto drivers and taxi wallahs seemed to be everywhere. So were the chai wallahs. These trains are not only linking and binding a billion people as one they are also providing livelihood to several millions, thought Sunil.

As far as Madurai was concerned, the Meenakshi temple was the centre of the Universe. Wherever you went, whatever you did, people referenced everything to the entrance to the temple. The temple had entrances facing all four directions. The whole complex spanned forty-five acres covering a huge rectangular area. There were fourteen Gopurams (towers) and these imposing structures could be seen from afar.

Their motel was on one of the outer streets running parallel to the famed Southern Entrance. The Southern Gopuram was the tallest of all the towers. Even at that time of the night, the streets were well lit around the temple, and there were people active on the streets. New York is the city that doesn't sleep they say but here too there were people going about their businesses in this hour be they just travellers or pilgrims or traders.

The clerk at the desk was half-asleep. Radhika did all the talking. She introduced Sunil as her brother. Sunil just smiled and nodded at everything that was said to him. Smile is the universal passport that gets you through many difficult situations.

When he asked for photo ID, Radhika gave hers. When he asked for Sunil's she went on an angry tirade in Tamil telling him off for taking too long and keeping them awake. They were tired and needed to sleep now. This brought about the desired result. The trembling clerk quickly gave them their keys and said he would deal with the rest of the formalities in the morning. Well that morning was never going to come, as the night shift person would be long gone off duty before anyone dared to disturb their sleep to ask for Sunil's ID.

16

It was nearly 11o'clock in the morning. They had settled in their respective rooms for the night. Radhika woke up at her usual time around 6.30. Her biological clock worked with precision irrespective of what time she went to bed. She was able to order tea to be brought up to the room. She managed to finish her morning ablutions and have her shower. She dressed up in a peacock green Mysore silk sari with red blouse. The sari had intricate design in different shades of green without being gaudy. When she looked in the mirror, she was mighty pleased. She had maintained her shape so well and with this sari, she looked very beautiful indeed.

She was hungry. She was not sure whether to wake Sunil up. The moment Ravana came into his life he has become a bloody Kumbakarna, she thought! This man is sleeping so late. How can he be guarding our borders? The enemies will love him, she thought. She was annoyed that he was holding them back. She wanted to go to the temple before breakfast. Now because of Sunil she had to fast for the morning. She could have gone on her own. But she wanted to show Sunil the jewel of Dravidian temple architecture. She was so proud of her heritage and wanted Sunil to imbibe in it.

Finally, close to noon she knocked on his door. "Wake up Mr Mishra. We are missing out on seeing this beautiful city and the wonderful temple!" It took a few knocks to awaken him from his slumber. It took him another hour for him to get ready. "It's like going out with a woman," she chided him. You spend too long on your make up!" as she sat on his bed waiting impatiently for him to finish up.

"You look gorgeous Radhi!" said Sunil as he combed his hair. "Praise won't get you anywhere Mister. It won't bring back the hours you wasted on sleeping!" She was in a hurry to go to the temple, and eat. They walked to the temple. Many people greeted them on the way. People thought they were husband and wife. They looked well matched for each other.

Many South Indian temples are built on the principles of women's liberation it would appear. This temple was dedicated to Goddess Meenakshi. Her male consort Sokkanatha played second fiddle. That's what the current temple attendees would think. The sixteenth century composition Thiruvilaiyadal purana talks extensively of the deeds of Sokkanatha. Perhaps the poet Paranjoti wanted to give importance to the male deity. In addition, the sanctum sanctorum for the main female goddesses were separate from that of their male consorts. It was like the modern families with independent working professional women where both the man and the woman had their own careers and their own circles of influence. Considering that the temples were built several hundred years ago, the society, or at least the higher echelons of the society, must have been quite progressive. When Sunil mentioned this Radhika was quite impressed. "Girl power," she said. "We are living in an era of girl power. You submit to it or perish!" She was quite serious about what she said. Being a professional woman, she viewed men as necessary nuisances rather than as providers and protectors. In fact, this aspect of Hinduism was a lot more advanced as far as women's rights were concerned compared to the other religions of that era.

They had to pay extra if they were to get closer darshan quicker. This is another phenomenon that has crept into South Indian temple culture. If you wanted shorter queues, you need to pay more. Sunil asked Radhika whether God or Goddess would look at the devotees quicker if they pay more. "No," said Radhika. "God looks at everyone equally. The social strata and economic disparity were created by man. Don't you know the story of Nandanar?"

"Not really. What is it?" asked Sunil. More than hearing the actual story, he was enjoying the expressive narration by Radhika. Her eyes would dance around and get bigger as she told the story with her emotional emphasis on certain aspects of the story.

"Nandanar was a Dalit devotee who wanted to see Nataraja in Chidambaram. Taking great pains and overcoming many obstacles he arrived at the great temple only to be told that he could not enter the precincts on account of being from the low caste. He was allowed to worship from the outside. But there was a large statue of Nandi the bull that was blocking his view.

"Having come all the way he could not see the Lord because of this Nandi. It was not exactly the bull in a china shop but nevertheless it was plonked well and truly in his visual path. He sang fervently "How nice it would be if the Nandi moved just a little bit." And lo and behold! The Nandi statue moved a little bit to allow him unobstructed view of his Lord. So that is a story told to illustrate that God does not discriminate between castes. It also tells you that it is your bhakti, not your status that moves God."

Having said this, she went on to say "From a practical point of view it is useful to have this 'easy pass' system because if you have to queue for several hours at each temple, like you do at Disney attractions, you will end up seeing only one or at the most two temples in a day. India is a populous country. There will be huge crowds at the bigger temples. There are many who go on temple tours. They may be NRIs, North Indian tourists or even tourists from outstations in Tamil Nadu. They want to see as many as possible within a short period of time. Once I saw eight famous temples in Tiruchirappalli, including the famed Srirangam, in one day. So depending on your purpose, this system offers flexibility. You can choose to stay in the queue for hours if that is part of your vow, or you may choose the quicker option. God is omnipresent and omnipotent. Spending more money won't win you special favours."

"Yes, even at the Vatican there is an easy pay quick option," said Sunil. Perhaps he wanted to show off to her about his travels. And Radhika loved these interactions with Sunil. He was well travelled, and knew a lot about every topic. That was one reason she felt attracted to this man, though she knew he did not belong to her.

They went into the Meenakshi sanctum. The priest thought they were a married couple. He did a pooja for them together, wishing them marital bliss. They looked at each other in a knowing way. This question about their relationship had been in the air for a while. Where were they going? What was the future for them? It was as if the priest had read their minds.

"Well?" asked Radhika. She enjoyed putting this man on the spot. She derived a pleasure from his discomfiture. Theirs was an unusual friendship. It was certainly not a normal relationship. Was it love? Were they prepared to commit to each other? Both had some feelings for each other. Was it just passing infatuation? Were they prepared to put their families through all the pain for their own selfishness? Especially Sunil had a lot to lose.

"Let's eat first," said Sunil, changing the topic. He was not ready yet. He knew that their relationship was like cottonwool waiting to catch fire. One of them only had to light the match. Both would be consumed in the fire in no time.

"Ok let's eat." Radhika asked him if he did not mind South Indian cuisine. They settled for masala dosa. In the afternoon, she wanted to show him Alagar malai. This was situated in a unique hillock on the outskirts of Madurai. They had to take a taxi drive past several kilometres of arid landscape. The hillock was unique. At the bottom level, it had the Vishnu temple, or the Alagar temple. At middle level, it had a famous Murugan temple, Pazhamudircholai. At this temple Radhika joked about Murugan's two wives. "Feel sorry for the poor guy!" said Sunil. "Having one wife is hard enough!"

If she was hinting, that put an end to that. After that, they walked to the top of the mountain. Here was a temple dedicated to a folk Goddess, Rakkayi. At this temple there was supposed to be a fountain that continued to flow during all seasons. People queued up to be splashed with this special holy water, which was said to have medicinal properties. They too queued. What was supposed to be sprinkling of water turned out to be a full-blown drench. As the lines moved around a central area, which contained the water baths the men standing atop on the walls of these baths poured water on them. Radhika got several bucketful's of water on her. Perhaps these men targeted the most beautiful woman in the crowd. Whatever their motivation was, the end result was that Radhika's sari and blouse were wet and completely transparent. It was like one of the wet tee shirt contests in the West. She looked very sexy with wet hair and transparent clothes showing off her inner wear. She was shy, which made her look sexier.

For the first time in their friendship, Sunil felt an arousal that made him feel hungry and guilty at the same time. She noticed that and this made her feel even more embarrassed. Her earlobes turned pink. She had a smile. He was not sure if that was an invitation or not.

They had to wait for her clothes to dry before going back to the taxi. The taxi driver would not want his seats to be messed up and Radhika did not want to be seen in this condition. They found a secluded spot to sit down. The irony is that when someone wants to be shielded away from prying eyes, they are also shielded away from the sun and the wind. Therefore, the sari took a while to dry. Sunil could not keep his eyes off her and after the initial furtive looks, started staring at her body directly. Radhika for her part, after getting over the initial hesitance, began to enjoy the warmth of his gaze.

They both knew that the ice had been broken and it would only be a matter of time before their relationship reached the next level. The water had actually fanned the fires of desire, instead of dousing them. It was barely possible to keep their hands off each other. "Radhi" whispered Sunil as he hugged and embraced her, lifting her face to plant a kiss on her lips.

"Not here" said Radhika. It was only a meek protest. She was trying to buy time as she tried to collect her thoughts. This was wrong. Both knew it was wrong from societal point of view. But from the biological point of view it was absolutely right. All these months of build-up had to have a release.

"Hey this is a public place. And it is sacrilege to do anything bad near the temple." Radhika's rational mind was kicking in.

"In Madurai there is no place that is not near a temple," said Sunil. It was true. Even if they went back to their rooms, they would not be far from the temple.

"At least we can go back to the motel," said Radhika. This confirmed her implicit consent. That settled the deal. "Ok let's go back then," said Sunil. Nothing else mattered at that time. He could hardly take his eyes off her on the return journey. He controlled the roaming hands to just placing his hand over her shoulder in a protective manner. There was nothing indecent in that. The driver thought they were husband and wife. He had seen a lot worse in his work.

As soon as they reached the motel, they rushed to her room. What happened in the next two hours was what has been happening since the time of Adam and Eve. It was natural progression of their relationship. There was no guilt and no expectations. It was gratification of a physical craving that both could not control any more.

If there were any guilt feelings, they evaporated as both realised how much they had wanted what had been just enacted. "Don't be afraid. I won't haunt you for the rest of your life. I am grateful for the happy times. I will not try to interfere in your marriage. I have other priorities." Radhika was back to her usual self, well in control of herself.

"I am worried," said Sunil. The unsaid meaning was not lost on Radhika. "Don't worry I am on the pill."

This was unexpected for Sunil. Does that mean she is in other relationships? Does it mean he had unrestricted license for the rest of the trip? He was confused. He had mixed feelings of happiness and jealousy at the same time.

Live for the moment, he said to himself. You have no right to be jealous. You cannot offer her the security of a marriage or family. You have no right to be possessive.

Radhika had not planned for this. She liked Sunil and loved his company. But she never intended for this to happen. She did not want to inflict pain on her friend. She did not want the spectre of two broken families to hang over her head for the rest of her life. However, she would be kidding if she said she did not enjoy what had just happened. These moments are to be savoured and not be spoilt by feelings of guilt, she told herself.

17

They left for Rameshwaram early in the morning. The plan was to reach Rameshwaram before 10 o'clock in the morning. The lush vegetation gave rise to shrub bush as they approached the Southern coast. Sunil had wanted to finish the job as soon as possible and return to Madurai Now he was not in any particular hurry. He wanted to drag this out. This was turning out to be quite a pleasurable trip. However, he told himself he should not lose sight of the primary purpose.

Rameshwaram is a town situated in Pamban Island, connected by to the mainland by a two kilometre long bridge. The bridge was the longest sea bridge in India for nearly a hundred years. It had a part that could be lifted to allow the passage of ships.

One of the most beloved sons of India, the late Dr Abdul Kalam, the former president, was born and raised in Rameshwaram. He was instrumental in the development of ballistic missiles and the development of India as a nuclear power. For all his achievements, Dr Kalam lived a simple man. He was a symbol of national unity. It was appropriate that the next development in India's defence capabilities should be associated with Rameshwaram, Sunil thought.

India and Sri Lanka are connected by a line of limestone shoals between Pamban Island on the Indian side and the Mannar Island on the Sri Lankan side. These could be seen from satellites and have the appearance of a mother and child reaching out to each other. At the closest points, the two countries are divided by only eighteen kilometres. At nights, lights could be seen on shores of both countries from certain points. Legend has it that this was the bridge built by Rama and his Vanara friends to facilitate troop movements from India in their invasion of Ravana's Sri Lanka. The shallow sea actually had a protective effect during the Boxing Day tsunami. While it makes sense to build a land bridge between the two countries, there is a proposal called Sethu Samudram project that envisages dredging of the sea between the two countries so that large ships could navigate these straits. This has met with protests from environmentalists from both sides. Whatever the environmental fallout of this dredging project may be, it is clear that the areas that were spared of the effects of the Tsunami will now be exposed to the devastating sea surge should this project go ahead.

Rameshwaram is one of the holiest Shiva temples in India. It contains one of the twelve Jyotirlingas, the most sacred of Shiva's symbols in India. It is the southernmost Jyotirlinga, the northernmost being at Kedarnath. The ambience was one of sacred power. The smell of the sea was all pervading. They decided that they will worship at the temple seeking guidance from the god to find what they came looking for. Sunil engaged a guide. All the talking was by Radhika, though the guide knew some Hindi.

"Looks like there are baths here too," said Radhika, her face reddening when she realised the import of what she had just said.

"Whoa! Wet tee shirt again!" said Sunil.

"Keep all bad thoughts out Mr Mishra. This is a holy temple!" said Radhika. They decided that they would not get distracted by the pleasures of the flesh until they find the information they came looking for.

Presently they had a sea bath at a place called Agni Theertha, to begin the ritual bath. After that, there were a series of twenty-two wells within the temple premises. They were asked to keep dry clothes and their cell phones in a separate water impermeable bag. At each bath, a Brahmin stood on top of a platform and poured water on them. The baths had to be taken in the exact prescribed sequence.

Radhika looked especially sexy in Sunil's eyes, in the light of the previous day's happenings. She knew the effect she was having on him. But no! They came on a mission and they needed to focus their attention on that.

Soon enough they were able to finish the baths and change into dry clothes. This time Radhika wore a lavender colour chudithar with simple but delicate embroidery. She looked resplendent in that. Perhaps the baths had washed away their sins, thought Sunil.

They asked the guide as well as the people manning the baths about the sea of Mandothari. No one seemed to know. Then the guide took them to a priest who appeared to be of higher status judging from the expensive silk garb. He did not know either. He was more interested in selling them a packaged moksha ritual. He said, "Rameshwaram is the place where many Hindus come to perform last rites of their relatives. You may have missed doing these for your loved ones in the past. I can do an all in one ritual which will cover all your ancestors and will also cover the ones who will die in the future, and this includes you too, for 3000 rupees. The normal cost is 5000 but as you look like a nice couple, I will do it at a discounted rate. This is only the cost of the yagna. The donation is in addition to that and you may add as much as you want."

When Radhika translated this to Sunil, she asked with a sarcastic smile "Do you really want to do this?"

"Are you crazy? The man wants me to do my own last rites!" Sunil was always skeptical of the expensive ritual that people get suckered into doing. If it makes people happy and provides livelihood to someone, why not do it? But doing one's own last ritual is taking this too far! Besides, they had already lost time and he did not want to waste another few hours on this activity, which was peripheral to their cause.

No one knew about Mandothari's Sea. No one knew about Ravana's yanthra. Then the driver suggested that they go to Kothandaramaswamy temple. Perhaps this is where the location of Ravana's secret will be revealed.

This was an ancient temple at the southernmost point of the island, Danushkodi. This was the only surviving major structure after a cyclone in 1964 washed away most of the buildings, the railway track and the station.

Until 1964, the ferry from Thalai Mannar, a point in Mannar Island off Sri Lanka docked at Danushkodi. Then passengers would go by train to Rameshwaram and the mainland. Many temples of historical and spiritual significance related to Ramayana were lost in the cyclone. This was one structure that withstood the assault of nature. Maybe there will be a clue there.

The temple was 13 km from Rameshwaram. It was crowded. Most of the devotees appeared to be form North India. Sunil and Radhika asked about Mandothari's Sea. One elderly man seemed to know about it. He said, "I know where it is. But you can't go there in a normal taxi."

He told them that vehicles could not go beyond a certain point unless they have four-wheel drive. Radhika and Sunil soon realised why this was so. Their driver was able to arrange another vehicle for the onward journey. It was one of the weirdest trips they had ever undertaken. It was breathtaking and scary at the same time. It was an experience of a life time.

The sandy beach stretched for as far as the eye could see. The sea was calm and gentle. The sky was blue and clear though there was darkness in the distance that told them they should not stay too long, as the weather could change any time.

The four-wheel drive traversed not just the sandy beach, it also had to actually get into the sea at some places where the arid plants with needle like leaves had grown in promontories right to the edge of the water and in some places in the water logged areas too. In order to avoid these areas the vehicles had to get into the sea. It was surreal to see many vehicles crisscrossing the shallow sea as though they were boats. It was not something either of them had seen before. The area was shallow but most vehicles had water covering most of the wheels. The drivers must have been very familiar with the terrain. One of the fundamental safety rules in times of floods is never to drive on water-covered surfaces because you won't know what the depth of the water. What if there was a sudden trench or quicksand in the sea? These drivers seemed to know their 'sea lanes' like the backs of their palms.

The driver thought he had an idea about where Mandothari's Sea was. He stopped and asked a few fishermen, and finally one of them knew where it was. He explained to the driver.

Mandothari was Ravana's long-suffering wife. Her unquestioning loyalty to her husband is hailed as a pinnacle of fidelity in Hindu lore. Unlike Ravana's brother Vibeeshana who deserted him when he knew his elder brother was in the wrong, Ravana's wife Mandothari stood by her husband until the end. Because of this Rama also treated her with great respect. He told her that he would grant a wish.

"Who will do my last rites, O' Rama? You have killed my husband!" lamented Mandothari. Rama told her that every time anyone performs the rites for their own kith and kin in this stretch of water, the benefit would accrue to her too. From that time onwards, this area was called Mandothari's sea. He asked them to have a dip there. How many times do they bathe in the day? They were reluctant but Radhika told Sunil "Hey if you want help from Ravana you better please Mandothari first!"

They had a quick bath. Fortunately, Radhika had brought a pair of shorts and a tee shirt. This served as beachwear. If the driver had not been waiting and if the weather had not changed, they may have frolicked in the water for a long time. The blackness in the distant horizon seemed to be getting closer. In addition, they were worried about the drive back.

They quickly changed back to their normal clothes and got back onto the vehicle. The next stop was a temple. The small temple was in a tiny islet surrounded on all sides by sea. There was seawater covering some of the floor of the temple for Shiva. The temple consisted of a small Linga and a Trishul only. There was a priest. He appeared to be in half trance. Otherwise, how can he be able to while away the time in this place so isolated from civilization?

The old priest looked at them kindly. Assuming they were husband and wife he wished them a long and blessed marital life. Then he offered to do an archana. While performing the archana he startled them when he recited "Om Ravana Yantharthipathiye Namaha." This was indeed the password that had been revealed to Sunil! The next line shocked Radhika even more. He said "Om Sivanolipatha Guhayaya Namaha."

The moment he uttered the words there was lightning and thunder. The heavens opened up suddenly. It rained very heavily. The sea level rose quickly. Within an hour they realised they were marooned. The driver said the four wheel couldn't be driven safely in these conditions. And it became dark. The sun was nowhere to be seen.

"You can't go in this weather. Please stay the night and go in the morning." The priest took them to another small islet. They were able to wade through waist deep water and reach there safely. The priest lived in a small hut. He had a wife and a small son. They were happy to share their meagre facilities. They gave their visitors change of clothes and some food.

Even after the rain stopped, the skies remained dark. The priest talked. "We have been looking after this temple generation after generation, for thousands of years may be."

Sunil probed "So Sir, you said Ravana Yantharthipathiye Namaha. This was the phrase I was told would unlock many mysteries! What is your connection with Ravana?"

"This whole place is steeped in Ramayana tradition. We believe that after Rama killed Ravana he worshipped Lord Shiva in this area. There is traditional folklore that Rama hid Ravana's Pushpaka Vimana somewhere in Lanka. Our mantras are supposed to reveal the secret. We believe that one day the right person will come here and decode the message."

Radhika asked, "You said 'Om Sivanolipatha Guhayaya Namaha.' What is the meaning of that?"

"As far as I know Sivanolipatha means the one who enlightened Shiva. Guha is Murugan. We know the story about how Murugan taught the Pranava mantra to Shiva. He is known as Sivaguru for that reason. So we have always understood this to be a reference to Murugan."

When they were alone Radhika told Sunil "Eureka! I think I have decoded the message."

"What is it?" asked Sunil. He was not sure what the conversation was about when Radhika spoke to the priest in Tamil.

"Sivanolipatham is the Tamil name for the famous Adam's Peak. Guha in Tamil can also mean a cave. I think the Pushpaka Vimana or a vital part of it, the yanthra, is hidden in a cave in Adam's Peak in Sri Lanka!"

The sudden change in the weather just when he uttered this, the fact that they were marooned and forced to stay the night, and the fact that the priest was able to converse with Radhika – they cannot all be coincidence, thought Sunil. He remembered the Hasalaka falls. When Ravana wants to convey a message, he will move mountains if necessary, thought Sunil.

Sunil fully agreed with Radhika that the next stop should be Adam's Peak, Sri Lanka.

Radhika said firmly that she was going with Sunil. After all, she was the one who picked up the clue. Sunil was not in a position to refuse. The only question was how much she needed to be told. In addition, should he introduce her to the air force chief and make her an official partner in this venture?

He had to decide, and decide very quickly. Now that they knew the location, he did not want to delay. Enemy spies would be trying to unearth the information. Sunil was quite certain that this was going to be a race against time.

18

Sunil took in the refreshing air at Nallathanni. Today was a day of relaxation. He had travelled here from Colombo via Hatton. Nestled among the mountains Nallathanni was the starting point of the most popular trail for climbing Adams Peak. This was a beautiful part of the world. How lucky are the people who live here? They enjoy the scenery and the fresh air all year round.

It had been three months since they returned from Rameshwaram. As if to punish him for his transgression, Lakshmy had to have a minor operation as soon as he returned. Sunil had to take charge of the entire household chores for two weeks. He was granted leave and supported in many ways by his employer. He was busy twenty-four seven, dropping children at school, music, dance, sports etc. He had no time to think of other things. He did not have time to talk to Radhika. Perhaps it was the guilt. Perhaps he was too scared of losing control over his life or maybe it was the superstition that his sins led to Lakshmy's illness. Sunil started avoiding Radhika. Besides, he did not want to lead her on. She had had enough complications in her life as of now. She could do without further issues.

He did mention taking her into their confidence and telling everything about the Pushpaka Vimana to the air force chief, but this was over ruled. This was very confidential information. Radhika knew some of it but not all. In fact, he was advised to cut off all ties with Radhika. He was given a new mobile number and the switchboard operators were asked not to put her calls through to Sunil. Though Sunil felt bad about it he thought this was for the good of the nation, and for all the individuals concerned. He fought the urge to cave in and obey the commands of his flesh. He chastised himself for thinking of her as an object. Yes, he was only thinking of the carnal pleasures. He had forgotten the contributions she had made in advancing the Pushpaka Vimana project. Above all, he had forgotten the emotional trauma he would have caused for a woman to be feeling she had been used and discarded. There was not even a good bye. No closure. He justified his actions to himself. Both knew there were no strings attached. She probably had other boyfriends. She was on the pill! He could transfer at least part of the responsibility to his organisation, which excluded her from the mission. But he knew, in his heart of hearts, that he owed her at least an explanation for this sudden turn of events.

The visit to Adams Peak was postponed due to other priorities. It took him an entire three months before the trip could be organised. So here he was, chilling out with a cold lager, looking at the distant mist covered mountain peak over the lush greenery of the montane forest. He would climb the mountain the next day. He did not have a clue as to where these caves were going to be. If Ravana wants his secret to be revealed, he will surely guide him.

The next morning he would climb. It was about a five-kilometre trek. Sunil was very fit. He reckoned he would do it in two hours. Climbing the peak was not what he came here for. He was here looking for clues to Ravana's Yanthra. Hopefully he will get guidance. Mr Ravana had helped the search all along. May be he was having an off day. Tomorrow he will be back on his guide duty. At least that was Sunil's hope.

Adams Peak has been a sacred place for thousands of years. It is mentioned in the Sinhala chronicle Mahavamsa and also the travel accounts of Ibn Battuta and the memoirs of Robert Knox. It had always been venerated. The Hindus believed that Lord Shiva's foot imprint is found at the top. Buddhists believe that Lord Buddha visited the peak and it was his footprint that was found at the top. Muslims and Christians believe it is their forefather Adam's footprint that is found there. Hence the name Adams peak. The Sinhala name Samanthakooda or Samanalakanda indicate the relationship to Saman, a Bodhisattva. The name for the mountain in common parlance is Sri Pada, while in Tamil it is called Sivanolipatham. These indicate the significance of the footprint to its lore. Because of these tens of thousands climb this mountain every year. Even if it was not done as a pilgrimage, the hike was a good holiday activity with reasonable though not too onerous physical challenge.

The footprint at the top is nearly six feet in length. The peak is more than 7000 feet from sea level. Though it was not the highest mountain in Sri Lanka, it was by far the most popular. The climb could be from the Northern or the Southern sides. There were six trails of which the Nallathanni trail was the most popular.

Sunil missed the company of Radhika. He knew that their relationship would go nowhere. Still she was a good travel companion. She was witty and sportive. Travelling with her to Rameshwaram was a great experience. Was he making a mistake by excluding her? Even the mountain climb would be a better experience if he had a companion.

He had to go to bed early. The hotel information officer had told him that everybody climbed in the wee hours of the morning so that they could be at the summit for the sunrise. The sunrise with the shadow of the mountain on one side was a sight to behold. Wherever there was a natural phenomenon, the sun provided additional vivid colours to the already spectacular landscape. Sunil remembered the time when he had been to Uluru in Australia. The sunset was especially wonderful as the mountain changed colours every few minutes as the sun made his journey downwards.

It was quite easy for Sunil to get to the top. The five-kilometre trek took only a couple of hours. In fact what held him back was really the crowd. As he approached the final ascent, the backlog from the top had slowed down the climb to a trickle. People were queuing to see the foot impression. He realised two things were wrong with his approach. Firstly climbing in the dark was hardly conducive for looking for anything leave alone something that he did not have a clue as to what it would look like. Secondly, the presence of large crowds meant he could not go into the bushes on the sides without raising suspicions of nefarious activity. In addition, he did not know the language. This was one time he rued the fact that Radhika was not with him. He was sure she would have thought about all these before starting the climb. He remembered the times when he would just get started on installing new gadgets, figuring out how to, by trial and error; Lakshmy would first read the manual and then do it all in one correct step. Having a female would certainly have enhanced the preplanning for this mission.

It was too late for all that now. There he was, at the top, looking in awe at this wonder of nature. If Ravana was going to help him, he had better do so quickly. He could not think of any other option. At the summit, some acquaintances that he had made during their upward journey told him they were climbing down the other side, the Southern aspect of the mountain. He could not do that. He had left his entire luggage in Nallathanni. If he climbed down the other side, he would end up in Ratnapura, a town that was about 4 hours travel by vehicle, from Nallathanni. He was in a quandary. Should he spend time at the summit and give Ravana more time to help him? Should he go back to Nallathanni accepting that this was a waste of time or should he go down to Ratnapura, and then collect his bags from Nallathanni later.

He sat on the side of the path on a small rock. The sun was well and truly up now. It was getting warmer. Fortunately, he had brought some water with him. There were plenty of small boutiques dotting the path all along. He had bought some water on the way up. Now he was hungry. What should have been a pleasant adventure is turning out to be an ordeal. He was slouched and was supporting his head on his palms. Today was not his day.

He felt a tap on his right shoulder. Suddenly he was brought back to reality from his melancholic world of self-pity. Who is this? He did not know anyone in this country, except Fernando. Yes! Fernando! Why didn't he enlist his help? He would have had some good suggestions. How could he have approached Fernando. Now the mission was shrouded in secrecy. It was not like the first time around, when he did not know what those objects were.

Or could it be Ravana? Ravana had always helped in indirect ways. He was never present in person. So why should it be any different this time. May be he changed his approach!

Presently he looked up to see who wanted to draw his attention. He couldn't believe his eyes. Oh my god! It was Radhika! And who is this person holding her hand? Has she already found a new boyfriend?

Radhika was dressed in jeans and tee shirt. The man with her – he was a hulk. He was also dressed in faded Denim and a white tee shirt. He was a six-footer at least. He was taller than Sunil. He had the build of a weight lifter. His biceps were bulging and he had tattoos in both forearms. He wore a copper bracelet around the right wrist. He had a thin moustache and a short beard. Both were wearing sunglasses. The first look said there was something evil in this man. Sunil decided not to prejudge this man. May be he was jealous. Has this man stolen Radhika from him? She was never his anyway. Sunil couldn't but compare this new man to himself. He was probably stronger than Sunil. In a hand-to-hand combat, he may beat Sunil. If they had a duel over Radhika, surely this man will win. The cave man instinct in Sunil was kicking in. Should he feel inferior to this person? We are not living in a stone age. We don't fight with bare hands anymore. Sunil Mishra, you are a Kargil veteran. You have seen combat. You are the best there is. The doubts quickly evaporated as Sunil regained his composure and self-confidence.

"Meet Sunil Mishra. Sunil, this is Dilip Kothari."

They shook their hands. Sunil noted the crushing handshake. It was not that he couldn't return in kind. But he didn't believe in showing off his strength in this manner. It is only the weak who need to project their power all the time, in order to conceal their insecurities.

"Dilip is a gentle giant. Don't get put off by his looks. He thinks he is a he man but he is a baby really." Radhika fondly fondled his hair. This very act annoyed Sunil. Why is she doing it in front of me? Surely, she wants to get back at me!

Radhika must have been savouring his discomfort. She had an evil grin. "Dilip was a good friend in school. Then we went our own ways. We reconnected recently." Then she told Dilip "Sunil is the husband of my friend Lakshmy. Remember the air force guy I talked about. This is the person." Turning towards Sunil, she said, "Dilip is an aeronautics engineer. I told him all about our adventure in Rameshwaram. We were due a holiday and we thought we should come here."

Has she told him everything? I never told her to keep it a secret. She is not obligated or sworn to secrecy, thought Sunil. In any case, she does not know about the involvement of Indian air force. This is what happens when you don't communicate fully. She knew only bits and pieces of information. She would have thought this was just an adventure. It was my fault for not keeping her in the loop.

Hell hath no fury like a woman scorned. So when I cut her off she must have resolved to check this out before I could, thought Sunil. He was not angry with Radhika. It was his own fault.

"We have been here for more than two weeks. We have done all the trails. Today we came up the Kuruwita Erathana trail. We took a route via Palabaddala. This is a much harder trail than the others are. In fact, we started yesterday. It was very arduous. We had to break journey overnight. This morning we bathed in a river called Seetha Gangula. As you know there are many streams starting from Adam's Peak that eventually join up to form two major rivers, the Kalu Ganga and Kelani Ganga. Seetha Gangula contributes to Kalu Ganga."

"While we were bathing I got a brain wave. The name Seetha Gangula is supposed to mean icy river. It was icy indeed. I shiver at the thought even now."

Saying this she actually shuddered. She must have had a ventricular ectopic thought Sunil. He had been trained in first aid. "Suddenly I thought Seetha is surely Rama's Sita! The answer had been staring us at our faces but we had been looking everywhere else! With that thought, I told Dilip we should explore this area. There were several large boulders and some caves in the vicinity. When we went near one of them, my heart raced. And indeed there was some metal object hidden in there. We have marked the area. We plan to go back to check it out. We came up to the summit just to complete the ascent from this side so we could boast that we have done all the trails. And guess what! I run into my boyfriend at the summit!" Radhika chuckled. This girl is a tease. So who was her boyfriend? What did she mean by that word anyway? Sunil was puzzled. He remembered that she was on the pill. Dilip must have been the reason for that.

"Why are you telling him about all that?" Dilip could not hide his annoyance at this intrusion.

"Sunil is the one who had the tryst with Ravana in the first place, silly! He works for our air force. He should be involved in this. I will tell you the more hands there are the merrier. Otherwise we won't be able to lift or carry this contraption even if we find it!"

"He is in the air force. That is the problem exactly. I work in the private sector and we are very efficient. We are motivated by profit. The moment you bring in someone who has worked for the government even for a day, they spoil the atmosphere. They are lazy. They are slow. And they work to rule!" Why is Dilip putting him down? He certainly felt threatened by the way Radhika opened up to Sunil. This was his territory. This was his girl. She had been under his spell for the last two weeks. Now this stranger comes and she is all over him!

It was clear to Radhika that the two men did not like each other. She had to enlist the help of both if this mission was to be a success. She would use her all charm to keep the peace. She had had a fling with Dilip in university. It was never serious. Dilip was not the kind of man who would take responsibility. When her marriage failed, she had tried to reconnect with old friends, both men and women. Dilip was one of them. They had fun. When Sunil ignored her calls, she found herself gravitating more and more towards Dilip. However, she knew this was not a serious relationship. He was a great asset when travelling. He seemed to have friends everywhere. Even in Sri Lanka, he seemed to have friends among the army and the police. That made their travel and stays easier.

They had arranged accommodation in a home stay in a nearby shop. This was arranged through Dilip's police friends. This place usually did not rent rooms. When Sunil asked what he would do to his belongings in Nallathanni, Radhika had a solution for that too. Since cell phone reception was not good in the area, she arranged to call the motel from the police post near Seetha Gangula. All of Sunil's travel documents including the passport were now in Nallathanni on the other side of the peak. Radhika's plan was to first complete their search and then go back to Nallathanni.

Again she had shown Sunil how level headed she was in her planning. Now he sincerely regretted not having brought her on board and shunning her for so long. He was grateful that she appeared to have forgiven him. However, he did not like the look of this new guy. Something in him was repugnant. Perhaps that's the kind of guy that girls get attracted to.

It took a while for the two men to adjust to the new realities and accept that they were in it together. They returned to their temporary accommodation in the evening. The weather was very bad and it was raining heavily. The visibility was very poor with the mist hanging over the area for the rest of the day. Radhika decided that they would not go out in search of the Yanthra that day. They had to sit by the fire lit by the house owner to keep warm. Their hands were numb and painful. They kept rubbing their hands in an attempt to warm them. Even a hot cup of plain tea, called kahata tasted like nectar.

19

They planned to resume their search in the morning. That night's sleeping arrangements were a bit awkward. It was obvious that Radhika and Dilip had shared a room. That was the only spare room in the house. They slept on mats on the floor. Radhika invited Sunil to share that room with them, much to the chagrin of Dilip.

Radhika was the livewire of the party and she kept telling Sunil about their university life. She also told Dilip about Sunil's exploits in Kargil. She also explained to Dilip how Sunil sucked her into this Ravana obsession. She carefully avoided telling that Sunil had been avoiding her lately. What was her motive? Why is she telling everything to the other man, each of them thought. What they thought was a secret between Radhika and each one of them was being shared with the other person.

Somehow, all fell asleep. Radhika woke up the others at dawn. She announced that she had a vivid dream. In the dream, she saw what appeared to be an aeroplane engine kept in a cave by a small stream, guarded by demons. She recognised the demons as the ones that had been visiting her in the dreams previously. The morning brought beautiful weather. The sunrise set the tone for the day. They had to manage with the meagre facilities at their makeshift accommodation. All were in good spirits and were ready for a day of search.

It was Radhika's hunch that brought them to Adams Peak. It was then her sudden impulse that was prompting them to search at Seetha Gangula. Now they were looking for the cave that she saw in her dream. What if these were all wrong? What if they were on a wild goose chase? Even if they returned empty handed, it would still have been worth spending time in this area. It was really a paradise on earth. The previous night's rain meant the river was in full flow, almost at bursting level. The sounds of gushing water cascading through the rocky terrain provided the ideal sound bites for the beautiful scene. The water was clear except for the bubbles. Black, brown and green were the colours of the riverbed, which was full of small moss covered rocks. The air was pregnant with water as clouds of mist moved across the clear blue sky. The trees were becoming shorter as they trekked up the hill. The visibility was a lot better than the previous day. Seetha Gangula was known to be a dangerous river. People were known to have drowned in this river. They had to watch each step.

The pebbles and rocks on the riverbed were slippery. The water was very cold. At its deepest, the water was about chest high. The currents were quite rapid. They decided not to waste time by bathing in the river. They would walk by the left bank going upstream to look for any cave that might resemble what was seen in Radhika's dreams.

The river had many branch points as they went up towards the headwaters as tributaries joined and then diverged, creating a lattice of water on the rocky terrain. "I am a leftist today," said Radhika as she decided to take the left turn at each branch point. On the return journey, they would be rightists, just like the many young men who start off as idealistic romantic socialists in university only to become arch capitalists as they grew older. They would have preferred to wear short pants for this trek but the cold weather did not allow that. They wore jeans that somewhat restricted their strides. In a way, it was good as short sure steps were what were needed.

"I crossed the river at one point in the dream. The caves were on the right bank." Radhika was trying to recreate the dream and find recognisable landmarks. The entrance to the main cave was hidden by a large boulder in the dream.

As they followed the river, they found themselves unable to walk on the banks as short shrubs and creepers made it impossible to walk by the river. As they tried to find their way, they found themselves going up and away from the river as it was now flowing through a ravine.

"How are we going to cross the river?" asked Radhika. They had to then climb down the rocks and walk across. The river was narrow at some points but they were not sure how deep the water was.

While they were wondering how to cross the river, they approached a hairpin bend to the left. As they took the turn, Dilip who was walking in front spotted it first! Yes, there was a hanging rope bridge! Some kind souls must have thought these three will come for the Yanthra at some point! "Now I remember we went across on a rope like this!" It was slowly coming back. Dreams are hard to remember when you wake up. The details come back to the memory in stages.

Sometimes the details just fade away. Radhika was not sure how they crossed the river. Was it a cable car? Was it a bridge? It didn't matter. The moment she saw the bridge she recognised it. It was deja vu. This was it!

They could only cross the bridge single file. It was old and Sunil was not sure if the rope had decayed or not. There were places where the rope had worn thin. He was reluctant to step on it. Radhika said, "I will go first! Ravana will protect us!" She stepped on the bridge without hesitation. The two men followed her lead.

Once they were on the other side Radhika asked them to turn left. They would have gone another hundred meters when she suddenly said, "I think we are close. The demons are playing in my head. We are very close.

There was a clearing and the river down below took a sharp turn to the left. Where they were, up on the elevation, there was some flat land, which contained some boulders. Then the rock face rose steeply. They went between the boulders and, low and behold! There was an entrance, which led in to a cave. It was pitch dark inside. Any sunlight that was shining through was blocked by the large rock. There was enough room only for them to squeeze through on their sides.

"We are very near. This is the one!" Radhika was trying to see as their eyes adjusted to the darkness. "We should have brought a light!" she lamented. How were they going to search in this one dark black recess?

"Call me prepared. Call me ready. Even Mr air force won't be carrying these!" Dilip Kothari took out a small flash light and a Swiss army knife from his pocket.

"You are a dear," said Radhika, tugging on his biceps. That's why I love to travel with you."

Sunil maintained an awkward silence. He was being bested by this hulk left right and centre. He just kept quiet. Dilip is the superman of the current times. What can ordinary mortals like Sunil Mishra do? They could only wish that supermen didn't show off and rub it in as much.

With the help of the light, they searched in the cave. After an hour or so they were about to give up when Radhika saw a small crack on the far sidewall of the cave. She put her eye to it. There was light coming from the other side. It looked different to sunlight. It had a bluish hue. It was as though someone had fixed a tube light on the other side. What was on the other side and how does one get there?

There must be a way. Surely, there is another recess in this cave. Where is the entrance? She sat there thinking. In the dream, she was saying a mantra. What was it? Yes, she said something and the engine appeared from nowhere.

"What is the mantra? There must be a password." Radhika was thinking aloud.

"Om Ravana Yantharthipathiye Namaha. Om Sivanolipatha Guhayaya Namaha." said Sunil. That was the only mantra he had heard in recent times.

The moment he said it there was an ear shattering noise and the ground shook violently. It was as though there was an earthquake. There was thunder and lightning inside the cave and it started to rain inside the cave. The rainwater began to collect first in a puddle and then started to rise, just like a tsunami, just steady incessant rise. The water quickly rose to knee level. They couldn't stand steadily in one place and were thrown about. Sunil fell down and nearly hurt his knee. There was no sign of any let up.

"Keep chanting Om Ravana Yantharthipathiye Namaha. Om Sivanolipatha Guhayaya Namaha. Don't stop!" screamed Radhika. She was frightened and shaken to the core. However, she had the presence of mind. If this mantra caused all this commotion, surely it would also restore calm. Both Sunil and Radhika kept chanting. After a couple of minutes everything stopped. There was pin drop silence. The shaking stopped and the water receded. Everything was as it was before, but there was a difference. The far side cave wall had opened up. Also, the boulder guarding the entrance had moved. There was unobstructed light coming from outside. Over and above it, there was another type of light illuminating the cave, with a shade of blue. The cave was much larger than before now that the inner compartment had been joined to the main cave to make it in to one big expansive room.

The luminous object looked like the engine of an aeroplane. It was shaped like a conical cylinder. It was about 5 feet long and 3 feet in maximum diameter, tapering towards the front. It was mounted on a platform with wheels.

"I think it is emitting radiation." Sunil was trying to think why it was glowing.

"Perhaps it is. But what can we do. We have already been exposed," said Radhika. "We have come all the way and found this quarry of ours. How can we leave it now?"

"I have had my children. What about you two?" said Sunil looking piercingly into Radhika's eyes. He wanted answers.

"I have had my children too. Don't look at me like that. Dilip and I are just friends. We are never going to marry are we Dilip?" Radhika said this nonchalantly. Dilip knew where he stood. Theirs was just a transient phase. Fellow travellers, literally. Both had other long-term plans.

"She treats me like a male organ, without any brains. I don't mind. I treat her the same."

"You are Mr Brawn. Sunil is Mr Brains. He is the one who remembered the mantra and saved the day for us, my dear Mr Muscle." Radhika was equal to the task when it came to jibes and put-downs. It was all done in the spirit of good humour. Or so they say.

Sunil couldn't understand their relationship. He had no right to know, he told himself. Radhika was too nice a girl to be given to this man, who looked dodgy from the time he first saw him.

There was no point in shying away from radiation, if any. They decided to roll the machine out. It moved surprisingly easy, considering that it had been there for tens of thousands of years. It was as though the wheels had been well-oiled and kept in readiness. It was not very heavy either. Ravanium, thought Sunil, the latest element and the new super metal.

"Do you think the bridge will hold its weight?" asked Sunil. "The only way to know is to try it isn't it?" said Dilip. He was in deep thought and his eyes were half closed. "I am thinking how are we going to take it on the other side, along those rocky foot paths?"

"Should we leave it here and come back with help?" Radhika was always very practical. "But in that case someone may take it!" Sunil protested. He knew this was a precious find. Also, he did not want any publicity. This was a secret mission.

"What is so important about it?" asked Dilip. "When Radhika said she was on a treasure hunt of some sort I joined in because it sounded like fun. In addition, I wanted to spend some quality time with her. That's why I joined her. This is just an engine. What's so special about it?"

"You don't know, Dilip. This is Ravana's engine. If we analyse how it works our air force will become the most powerful force in the world. Am I correct, Sunil?" Radhika said this with pride in her eyes. She looked to Sunil for confirmation. Though she knew they had stumbled upon some great discovery, she was not privy to all the information.

Sunil did not answer her. He did not want the confidential details to be discussed in front of this man who looked like a misfit in the society in his eyes.

"Ok let's get going before the weather turns bad. Let's get to the other side. I have army contacts. I will get help to haul this machine to Colombo." Dilip was trying to get control of the situation. He was thinking fast. He did not like Sunil. Not the least because Radhika seemed to have a soft corner for him. He wanted to exclude Sunil from this project. After all, it was Radhika and Dilip who searched physically on all sides of Adams Peak. Why should he then surrender the spoils to this man?

At this point in time, Dilip took the lead. He was the strongest of the three. He would haul the machine and cross first. Radhika should follow him to make sure the sides of the machine did not get caught in the balustrade rope. The deck of the bridge was paved with wooden slats and the wheels should roll without too much trouble. It was the sides that he was worried about.

His plan seemed good. Sunil would stay on the far side, as the bridge may not hold all of them plus the machine. Though the wheel-mounted machine was easy enough to pull, they were not sure how much it weighed. It made sense not to overload the bridge.

With a few hiccups, Dilip reached the other side, with Radhika tailing behind, the machine in the middle.

As soon as he got to the other side, Dilip's demeanour changed. He quickly tried to pull the machine to his side. Then he took the Swiss army knife and started to cut the rope at the anchor points.

"Stop! Are you crazy? What are you doing?" Screamed Radhika. Whatever he was doing could not be good.

"You bitch! Either you can choose to go with that man who is trying to steal this machine for the Indian air force or you can come with me. You have known me for years and quite intimately too! But you never asked me. I tell you now. I converted to Islam a couple of years ago. My name is Dilshad Kader. You are a shameless infidel bitch. If you want to come with me, I will show you heaven. But don't think I will marry you unless you convert."

"What are you saying?" Radhika's tone was weak. The voice was hardly audible. This explained many of the changes of physical appearance and mannerisms. It also explained why he would go incognito many times a day. Presumably, he was praying five times. She liked him as a friend. She could count on him for physical side of things. He was quite dominant. She didn't mind that. Would she leave her family and her community for him? He did sound strange now. He was trying to cut the bridge off! This is evil! What is his motive?

"Listen bitch! I have connections with ISI in Pakistan. I have friends among the army here. We can sell this engine for millions of dollars. We can live in huge mansions in Los Angeles. We can move among the Hollywood elites. If you choose him, all he can give you is may be a Bharat Rathna and a few paisas. He is a married man. He can't even give you a status in society."

"This machine belongs to Sri Lanka. Why should he be allowed to steal it for India? My friends in the army will love me if I prevent this threat."

Sunil realised that he had no time to waste. Unless he crossed immediately, he would be left stranded on the other side. If the bridge gives while he was on it he would die. No one could physically survive a fall from this height onto the rocky bottom. It would be like falling off a bungee jump.

He did not mind dying. He had seen combat. He had seen death at close quarters. He had his family to think about but that was not his first priority. This machine is going to dominate the world for the next fifty years. He could not allow that to fall in the hands of the enemy.

He had to speak out. Even as he prepared to make a dash for the other side, he addressed Radhika. "Radhi! I am an Indian and I am a proud Indian. We live in the best country in the world. We have a duty to defend our way of life and the future of our kids. If you go with him, you will lead a hedonistic life and drown in the pleasures of the flesh. No amount of money can buy you the feeling that you have done the right thing for your country. I may have hurt or ignored you and I can explain everything when we get an opportunity. Right now we have to stop him!

"Sure this machine is found in Sri Lanka. But Sri Lanka doesn't have the money or the infrastructure to develop this. All they can do is to sell it to a foreign country, i.e. if this man has not already lined up a private deal for himself. Since the time of Ramayana Sri Lanka and India are intimately related to each other. You saw how the Sethu Bridge connects the two countries. The landscape on both sides of Palk Straits is almost the same. If you suddenly wake up on one side of the sea, you won't know which side you are on. That is how similar they are. Now Ravana has been feeling guilty about Sita. He loved Sita. Probably she liked him too. You may call it Stockholm syndrome. Whatever the case may be Ravana wants to help Sita's people. He knows that a strong India will protect Sri Lanka. Together they will stand. And divided they will fall."

Saying this he made a dash for the other side. He had only a few seconds before the bridge collapsed. It was now or never. Even if he didn't make it to the other side he wanted Radhika to do what was right for her country. Hence his words to her, even though it wasted some precious moments.

For Radhika the choice was easy. From her childhood, she had loved her country. If it were a choice between money and her country, she would choose her country without batting an eyelid. It was a no brainer. The only issue here was Dilip. This would mean parting of ways permanently. She liked him. She also knew that Sunil would never be able to give her a life of matrimony. She did not want to inflict pain on her friend Lakshmy and her children. However, here the choice was not between Dilip and Sunil. It was between Dilip and Mother India. There was no choice really. There was only one way she could decide!

Radhika pulled the machine with all her energy and tried to walk backwards towards the centre of the bridge. Sunil was trying to come from the other side. Radhika's move was actually counterproductive on several counts. With her moving towards the centre of the bridge, the centre of gravity shifted and the rope that was already half severed completely gave way with a huge noise. The vibrations of two people and the machine rushing in opposite directions caused the bridge to sway up and down vigorously, hastening of the snapping of the rope. Radhika and the machine coming towards him negated any slim chance that Sunil had of crossing the distance before the bridge collapsed.

In reality, Sunil's little motivational speech actually served to conspire against them. Sometimes it is better to show in action before speaking. But it was too late for them. Lock stock and barrel both Radhika and Sunil, not to mention Ravana's engine, headed fast hurtling down at g-force, down the valley towards the rocks and the raging waters.

What were the last thoughts in their minds? Is this the prize for patriotism they would have thought. Is this the price for preventing this lethal machine from falling into the wrong hands they would have thought. Perhaps they would have felt sorry for Ravana. After all his efforts in trying to unveil the hidden machine, it is going to be shattered into a million pieces. Even the great Ravana is fallible. Would they have thought about the children? Would Sunil have thought about Lakshmy? Or would he have thought about the air force. Will they give him a posthumous award for bravery? They wouldn't even know that he died. Oh what happened to the cell phone given by the air force chief? That was probably going towards its watery grave faster than Sunil.

A sad end to a brave tale. The villain survived. May be that was Ravana's way of taking revenge.

20

Navathenna!" The sentry stopped the van at gunpoint. There were six soldiers in fatigues. They had AK 47 rifles pointed at the driver. The driver, Nilamdeen was a bit puzzled by the unusual security in the roads. Not since the end of the war had he been stopped so many times. What was going on? Has there been an attack? He was confused. He was on his usual run from Ratnapura to Colombo. His boss had assigned him to drive these guests to his Colombo branch.

"Mokadda kalabale ralahami?" Nilamdeen started to ask the soldiers what was wrong. "Kata vahanna yako!" shouted the soldier, asking him to shut up.

At that time there was another man with them. He was in civilian clothes. He said "Aslamu alaikkum" noticing the fez cap on Nilamdeen's head. The familiar voice sent shivers down the occupants' spine. They looked at each other and remained silent.

The soldiers looked inside. Seeing two Muslim women wearing abhaya, they just waved them by. The ladies were covered from head to toe, with only the eyes being open to the world through slits. The man in civilian clothes wanted to inspect the cargo in the back of the Hiace van. Seeing that it was all boxes and boxes of clothes he closed the door and waved them by.

That was the closest they came to meeting their tormentor since the escape from Seetha Gangula. Yes, it was Dilip who was in civilian clothes. Fortunately, they were not asked to get down. Seeing a Muslim driver with two women passenger,s they decided these were not the persons they were looking for.

It was Sunil and Radhika in the passenger seats. They were still in awe as to how they cheated death. The last thing they remembered was that fall. That disastrous fall from the bridge. Both of them must have fainted.

When they came to, they were floating in the middle of a river, which they came to know was Kalu Ganga. They were in a place called Ratnapura. They were floating on Ravana's Engine. They couldn't figure out how they ended up there. Nor could they understand how a metal engine mounted on a base could float, that too with two people on board.

A kind fisherman helped them to get ashore. When she heard that they were in a place called Ratnapura, Radhika was overjoyed. Her father owned a jewellery shop. He had business dealings with a Muslim gentleman Haji Pichai Mohideen in Tuticorin. Haji Mohideen had businesses in India and Sri Lanka. He had operations in Ratnapura, Colombo, Chennai and Tuticorin. He was one of the people who had relatives in India and Sri Lanka. There are many families who spend half the year in Chennai and the other half in Sri Lanka, like the legendary King Vikramaditya. Ratnapura was the gem capital of Sri Lanka. It was rumoured that there were gems strewn all across the area that even sifting through a small area of shallow earth may produce a handful of gems. Sapphire was one of the most sought after stones that was especially common in the area.

As a child, Radhika had visited Ratnapura with her father. She had stayed as a guest of Haji Mohideen. So she was overjoyed when she heard they were in Ratnapura. She asked for Haji's shop and was promptly taken there. The rest was easy as the businessman was delighted to see his friend's daughter, though in unusual circumstances.

Radhika and Sunil had to explain the situation to a limited extent. The astute businessman understood that they had to transport contraband to India, in addition to getting safe passage for themselves. Sunil did not want to go through official channels, as that would spark a diplomatic incident if the Sri Lankan government came to know that they were removing an artefact that was tens of thousands of years old. They did not tell him of the military significance of the object.

Smuggling was not a big deal for the Haji. That was an everyday occurrence. Since the end of the civil war, the naval patrols had reduced drastically. There were many routes. The preferred route was Negombo to Tuticorin.

The Hamilton Canal connected Colombo to Negombo. Dotted with sandy beaches, there were some places in Negombo where the vegetation went right onto the waterfront. These areas provided cover for the clandestine activities. The navy turned a Nelsonian eye towards small time smugglers. They were interested only in the Tigers. With the end of the civil war, this surveillance too was eased to a large extent.

Radhika and Sunil were dressed in wet suits. There were two others, the captain and the helmsman. They also wore wetsuits. They were masked. Both were tall and hefty men. "They are dear and near to me. Look after them," said the Haji. The men nodded in assent. They did not speak. Once Haji Mohideen handed them over to the boatmen they loaded the boat with the cargo for the day including Ravana's engine. The engine was neatly wrapped in polythene, as were the rest of the goods. The fibreglass boat was about 10 metres long. It was fitted with two outboard motors in addition to the regular motor.

The boatmen handed them life jackets that they had to wear during the entire journey. The two passengers were asked to sit near the front of the boat, which was partially covered. Under the cover of darkness, they set out, among the hundreds of fishing boats that ventured out every night. The boats would be fishing all-night and return at dawn.

Once they were well and truly in mid sea, the smugglers broke out from the group of fishing boats and made their dash for India. The ocean was rough. The boat was quite small and went up and down with the waves, tossing and turning all the time.

They held on to the handrail. The cargo had been secured by ropes. This was quite a routine operation for the smugglers. For Radhika and Sunil this was a very scary and strange experience. About an hour into their journey, the helmsman took off his mask. "Look who we have here," he said, laughing menacingly at the couple. He had a short knife that he waved threateningly at Sunil.

Yes, it was Dilip! Radhika did think his build was similar to Dilip's when she first saw him. But she had reassured herself that it was not possible for the brigand to turn up in her father's friend's service. Now it was clear that this was indeed none other than the villain himself.

Waving the knife close to Sunil's face he said "You infidel! You brain washed this bitch and stole her away from me. I will punish her later. But now I shall finish you off."

He was enjoying the taunting. This was cat and mouse play. He wanted to draw it out a bit. He had a few more hours to go. His companion would steer the boat. He was going to bully the two before killing Sunil. Then he would deal with Radhika. He would first torture her. Then he would bully her into submission and make her his sex slave. He would teach the bitch not to mess with him. By the time he was done with her, she would know her place in this world.

Sunil was thinking fast. If he resisted, they would all go down to the ocean's floor. At least the engine would not fall into hostile hands. If he did not resist at least Radhika would be spared. She may get a chance to turn the tables at the opportune moment. But what was the guarantee that Radhika would not be killed too.

Momentarily he heard a thud. "Thwack" was the sound. He turned around to see Dilip was slapping Radhika. "Leave her alone. Your grouse is with me. Kill me if you want."

"I will kill you. But this bitch needs to be disciplined." Sunil looked at Radhika. There were tears in her eyes. Her cheeks were red. She was gritting her teeth in an attempt to hold back the tears. She was breathing heavy.

"Tell her to do as I say," Dilip said. He wanted to humiliate both by getting them to do bad things to each other. He gave her a piece of nylon rope and asked her to tie Sunil's hands behind his back. Sunil told her not to resist. After this Dilip asked Sunil to kneel on the floor of the boat. He slapped him. He slapped him again.

This was the ultimate humiliation. He looked at Radhika. She had also been made to kneel down. Dilip tied her hands behind her back. She was sobbing. There was a look of abject terror in her eyes.

Dilip was not taking chances. He was following the rules of the ideal tormentor. To defeat the victims psychologically and break their resistance was his first goal. First, divide the victims. Make them feel that some have a chance to escape. Get the one who is going to die to tell the potential survivor to obey. Yes, the first victim would think that they are helping the latter by asking them not to resist. Then get one to incapacitate the other – to get them to bind or gag their companion. Now the bully has to deal with only half of their adversary, with the other half already been rendered useless. By this time, the resistance would have evaporated completely.

This way was much easier than trying to fight both at the same time. He knew that if they had a fight mid sea, while trying to control the boat at the same time, they would all die. The boat would have capsized, no doubt.

When will he slit Sunil's throat. He wanted to harass Radhika more before he played the end game. It will benefit his long term plans to completely destroy her ego now. Then he could enslave her for the rest of her life. He made a shallow slash on Sunil's neck. In spite of the wet suit blood started to drip. Radhika was a doctor. She knew that if the knife went any deeper it would cut his jugular vein or carotid artery. Any other person would have fainted at the sight of blood. Radhika was a doctor. The sight and smell of blood only made her think faster. What could she do? Their hands were bound. They were in the middle of the Indian Ocean. This was the ocean that swallowed hundreds of thousands during the Boxing Day tsunami. Accommodating just two more won't be a problem for God Varuna.

Then she remembered. The moment she thought of Varuna she remembered Ravana. "Om Ravana Yantharthipathiye Namaha. Om Sivanolipatha Guhayaya Namaha."

Suddenly the ocean swelled up. There was a huge wave. The moment the boat came down, it went up again in another huge wave. All of the occupants were tossed into the water. The boat broke into pieces. Then there was silence. Instantly the sea was calm again. There was no sign of anything or anyone in the water.

21

It was a secret ceremony at Rastrapathi Bhawan. There was no fanfare. Only a few people attended. The President was there as was the Prime Minister, the entire cabinet and the Leader of the Opposition. The armed forces chiefs were present. The families of Radhika and Sunil were there. Dr Rangarajan was also in attendance.

The air force chief spoke first. After going through the protocol of addressing the Executive he said "Friends we have gathered here to felicitate Air Vice Marshal Sunil Mishra and Dr Radhika Rao. They have risked their lives many times to uncover major secrets which will help us to augment our military capabilities to a level where no other country can compete with us for the next fifty years."

"Ramayana was a legend, we believed till now. We know now that Ravana really existed. Ravana has been overcome by remorse about what he did to Sita. To redress the wrong he has revealed, through these two courageous people, the entire workings of his Pushpaka Vimana. We believe that further advances on this would enable us to dominate the skies. It will also help in satellite technology. Even exploration and colonisation of Mars is a possibility. We believe that Ravana used his Vimana for inter galactic travel.

"We have found a new element, Ravanium, which is stronger and lighter than all known metals. It has opened the possibility of finding a whole new class of elements. The Periodic Table has to be radically revised.

"We have also discovered that Ravana used Metamaterials to create an invisibility cloak around his vehicle. We know that we can hide our aircraft not only from the naked eye but also radars and satellites.

"We have also uncovered a new polymer which we shall call Ravanalon which will help not only military technology but will revolutionize every aspect of life."

"And we now have an engine that uses nuclear fusion that is small enough to be fitted on to air craft. This is the biggest prize of all. With this engine, it would be possible to go to Mars in a few days' time in the not too distant future."

"Both these courageous and patriotic individuals have put their lives in peril to achieve this. They will be awarded the appropriate civilian and military awards in due course. Sunil Mishra has been promoted in ranks already. They will also receive lifelong pension commensurate with their contributions. We don't have peerage like in the UK. Otherwise we would have made them Lord and Dame respectively."

Lakshmy looked at her husband with pride. It had taken a while to convince her why he ended up going to Rameshwaram and Sri Lanka with Radhika. Now all was forgiven and all was well, in the patriotic fervour of the moment.

Radhika and Sunil were found in mid sea by the fishermen from Rameshwaram, floating on Ravana's engine. They did not remember what happened after they fell in the ocean. No one saw Dilip again.

"I wanna pee. I wanna pee, Dad!" said Ajay. He had
been waiting at the ceremony for hours without
wanting to miss a minute. It all ended how it started.
Another cycle of life.

THE END

Acknowledgements

Thank you to my dear wife Dr. Mythily Ramanathan MD for supporting me through the thick and thin of life.

Thank you to my aunt Parvathi Nagasundaram for inculcating English in me at a very early age, giving me the tools to rub shoulders with native speakers.

I thank Dr Steven Lev MD for creating the beautiful cover for this edition.

www.ingramcontent.com/pod-product-compliance
Lightning Source LLC
Chambersburg PA
CBHW051254250626
47155CB00009B/3292